A Trail Untamed

Wagon Train Matches

Lacy Williams

Chapter One

They were everywhere.

August Mason sat tall in the saddle on top of his buckskin mare as dawn's silver light filtered over the horizon. His breath frosted on the morning air, but he knew the cool wouldn't last. By noon, he'd be shedding his slicker. It was almost June.

He was the only rider in sight. Alone out here, where no distractions meant he could hear himself think.

And what he thought was the herd of buffalo that stretched as far as the eye could see was beautiful—but deadly. The enormous animals seemed peaceful enough as they grazed the long prairie grasses, but he'd heard stories of a mother buffalo stomping a dog to death when she had felt threatened.

There were a lot of kids in the wagon train. He would tell Hollis that everyone needed to keep their distance from the buffalo.

Hollis Tremblay, the wagon master, should be out here himself. August had been scouting with him since

1

the start of their journey. But Hollis had been gravely injured when a recent tornado had destroyed several wagons from their train. The wagon master's terrible head injury had kept him flat on his back. The man couldn't sit a horse without the plague of dizzy spells and headaches. He'd asked August to be his eyes, scout the route ahead and give daily reports on the best way to traverse the difficult terrain.

But he had asked more than that.

He'd asked August to be one of the captains, men appointed to leadership by the company, tasked with keeping the peace, settling disagreements between travelers, and setting the watch at night.

August had declined.

Their wagon train had left Independence, Missouri six weeks ago. By August's calculations, they were currently somewhere in the Nebraska Territory. In these six weeks, he'd witnessed more altercations between travelers than he cared to think about.

People were selfish and unkind, and the dangerous journey and monotonous conditions only seemed to magnify their natural faults.

A lot of folks were scared.

And scared people made bad decisions.

He knew enough about making those kinds of decisions himself.

Pushing away thoughts of the past, he rode out another two miles, urging his horse into a gallop that the buckskin gave him. Then he followed his sense of direction as he traversed a different trail. Probably a deer track, faint through the woods.

August was alert for any sign that something wasn't

2

right. A broken twig could mean someone had traveled through here recently. He'd seen scat from coyotes, deer, buffalo, raccoon. No sign of bear or wolves in the past weeks, but they'd be entering bear country soon enough.

He forded the river in a different spot than he had in the near-dark just before dawn. Dismounted, water streaming from his pants and slicker, and walked up and down the creek bed, attempting to judge whether a wagon wheel would get stuck in the rocky, sandy soil. He didn't much like the feeling that a company of over two hundred souls was depending on him for their safety.

As he came up out of the river bottom, he was afforded a glimpse of the circled wagons, their white canvas tops like a beacon amongst the greens and yellows of the prairie grasses.

There was movement around camp. Men hitched oxen to the wagons or saddled up. Inside the ring of wagons, he knew women would be tending cookfires for breakfast or packing up their wagons. Making preparations to leave.

On foot now, he approached his half-brother, Leo Spencer, and Leo's half-brother, Collin Spencer, as they saddled their mounts.

August's father had been married to Leo and Alice's mother but had walked out on the family when Leo was a tot. He'd gone West. All the way to California, where he'd married August and Owen's mother. August and his brother hadn't known about Leo and Alice until their father's deathbed admission. After Pa had passed, Owen insisted the right thing to do was find their long-lost siblings and try to make things right—share the inheritance that Pa had left behind.

Alice had been welcoming. But Leo had wanted nothing to do with them. Leo had had troubles of his own. His younger half-brother Coop, Collin's twin, was a troublemaker, and they'd been in a hurry to leave New Jersey. It had taken weeks of working together on the wagon train for Leo to stop looking at Owen and August with a suspicious glare.

August still wasn't sure whether his older half-brother wanted them around, wanted the added protection of two strong men for his new wife and her very young sister.

Which is why he intended to walk past the two men without saying hello.

He could overhear their hushed conversation though he kept his head tilted so his hat blocked them out of his sight.

"I don't know where he's getting the whiskey." That was Leo, complaint audible in what was barely more than a grunt.

"I'll talk to him again." Collin was the peacemaker in their family dynamic. It was easy to hear the placating tone in his voice.

"Do you think Alice is helping him hide it?"

"Why would she—?"

"Morning," Leo called out.

August glanced over to find Leo looking right at him while Leo tightened the cinch on his saddle.

Collin's eyes darted between the two men. He finished adjusting his stirrup. "I need to go check on Stella."

August made his living as a trapper. He spent days on end in the woods. He'd honed his senses to be able to detect the faintest shift in the wind or slightest rustle in the undergrowth. Which is why his shoulders tightened at the undercurrent of tension between him and Leo and Collin.

Leo and Collin shared a closeness that August wasn't part of. And not knowing whether he was welcome in their close-knit family made him uncomfortable.

Enough to say, "I've got to talk to Owen. Give him my report."

"That can wait." Alice appeared, having crossed the space between the wagons and where he stood near the picketed horses. "Breakfast," she said in her matter-of-fact manner, holding out a tin plate heaped with flapjacks and fried ham.

He never had any question where he stood with Alice. She was an open book. A firecracker. And he knew enough about her that he took the plate. She was stubborn enough to follow him around until he ate what she gave him.

He liked her. And it was easier to turn in her direction and let Leo and Collin finish their murmured conversation.

"Do you even sleep?" she asked, one hand propped on her hip.

"Of course." He spoke around a bite of flapjack.

"I don't believe it. You're either on watch or out scouting before any of the rest of us wake up." She was glaring at him a little.

Was this what having a sister was like?

"I sleep." Not much. He worried about the safety of their wagon train. In some ways it was easier to scout out potential dangers than to quiet his mind while lying in

5

his bedroll worrying about all the things that could kill them out here.

She was still watching him. He swallowed the bite in his mouth. "How's Felicity?"

Felicity was another of the travelers, a single woman who had paired up with another young woman, Abigail, to go West together. They'd faced some misfortune, namely the twister that had ripped their wagon apart and injured Felicity.

"Why don't you ask her yourself?"

There was some spark in Alice's eyes. Curiosity maybe. Or orneriness. He couldn't tell.

He bent his face over the plate, hoping it would hide the slight heat he felt creeping into his cheeks.

Felicity's voice box had been damaged when her wagon nearly crushed her. She couldn't speak. And the fact that she had a hard time communicating made him tongue-tied and awkward around her. She'd thought he was sweet on Alice, for heaven's sake.

Owen waving to him from near their wagon was a relief. Now he could escape Alice's nosy interrogation.

"I gotta go." He passed her the plate, now empty. Thought better of just running off. Leaned over to buss her cheek with a kiss. "Thanks."

"You'd better sleep tonight," she called after him.

Felicity Vacker woke to the sounds of camp breaking.

Light filtered through the small gap in the canvas tent where she and Abigail had been sleeping these past few days.

She'd overslept. Again.

She'd asked Abigail to wake her—

Felicity rolled over, sucking in a desperate breath when her bruised ribs flared with a pain that felt like a tongue of fire licking down her left side.

She wanted to curl into a ball, let the tears that pricked at her eyes roll down her cheeks and just wail.

But she couldn't.

She dug her fingertips into the bedroll and pushed up with her arms until she was in a sitting position.

It wasn't any better. The pain was constant, and enough to take her breath away.

A week ago, the pioneers had been caught in a terrible storm. Several wagons had been decimated by a tornado—including Felicity and Abigail's wagon, with Felicity inside it.

She'd nearly been crushed by the wreckage, but she'd lived. They didn't have a doctor on the wagon train, but one of the young women had some training as a healer. She'd diagnosed Felicity with busted ribs. The injury made every movement painful.

But they were only a month into the two-thousand-mile journey and their company couldn't afford any delays. Which meant Felicity traveled on with the rest, though she'd been relegated to riding in a wagon instead of walking. Walking was painful, each step jarring her ribs.

Voices murmured outside the tent.

"Anyone think to wake Felicity? They're gonna blow the bugle before long."

She recognized the steady cadence of August Mason's voice. He'd been the one to find her and Abigail after the terrible storm. She would've still been trapped under the broken pieces of the wagon if he hadn't lifted them free.

Someone answered him, the second female voice farther away, and she couldn't make out who was speaking.

"She still in there?" he asked, his voice closer now. "We need to pack up the tent."

She opened her mouth in a frantic moment of modesty. She was still wearing her nightdress. It would be highly inappropriate for him to pull back the flap. But no words emerged. Her voice remained useless. Gone.

His shadow fell over the split in the canvas door.

And at the last moment, she clapped twice.

His shadow froze.

"That you, Felicity?"

She clapped twice more.

She hadn't known August before he'd saved her, other than as a face amongst the other travelers. Since then, she and Abigail had been taken in by August and his brother, Owen, and by association, with their other family.

Now she knew August was not only intelligent, but he noticed things. Small things.

"We're getting close to time to move out," he said now. "Take a few minutes and I'll come back to break down the tent, all right?"

She clapped twice more. He seemed satisfied with that because his shadow disappeared from in front of the tent.

It took far longer than it should've for her to slip the nightdress over her head and put on her dress instead. Lifting her arms was agony. She couldn't help the tear that fell, but she whisked it away with her wrist.

She hurried out of the tent with the bedroll in disarray, which once would've frustrated her, but with her current limitations, she had no choice. She found a private place to relieve herself and splashed her face with water at the creek before picking her way step by painful step back to the wagons.

Nearly everything was put away when she got back. Abigail, in her yellow gingham dress, stood on a crate, her dark hair pulled back behind her head and barely visible from where she stood with her shoulders inside the wagon. Did she need help? Maybe Felicity could offer assistance.

She neared the wagon and heard Abigail counting quietly.

"Not enough," came Abigail's words through the canvas covering.

Was Abigail counting the meager stores of food they had left in their wagon? After riding in the back of the conveyance for days, Felicity had come to know almost too well what little they had.

Abigail stepped down off the crate and turned, coming face to face with Felicity. Abigail's light brown skin and dark eyes were shadowed with realization. They didn't have enough food supplies to make it to Oregon. The twister had decimated their stores.

No food. It took a few moments for Felicity to make Abigail understand with rudimentary hand gestures.

Neither one of them had acknowledged just how deep their misfortune was before this moment.

Abigail shored up a smile. It even looked real. "We'll be all right. God will provide."

Felicity's stomach twisted.

She hadn't known Abigail before the start of their journey. They'd both arrived in Independence, Missouri, looking for a partner for the journey west. The wagon master, Hollis Tremblay, had connected them.

It had become clear on the first day that Abigail was Felicity's complete opposite. She sang her way through backbreaking chores, always had a smile for anyone she met, and never stopped talking.

It should've bothered Felicity, but she'd been fond of Abigail from the very start. But right in this moment, Abigail's hopeful attitude just made the heaviness inside Felicity more crushing.

There were no supply stores along this route. Only forts filled with soldiers. And *if* they had food supplies to spare, like flour and coffee and salt, the prices would be exorbitant.

Felicity and Abigail had spent every last cent to pay for the supplies they'd lost.

There was no bright side to this.

Felicity didn't know how they would survive.

And she wasn't nearly as certain as Abigail was that God would provide. He hadn't done so for Felicity when she'd needed Him the most.

The bugle sounded from across camp. Abigail nodded. "I'd best check on Hollis before we leave."

Felicity was left to stare at the crate and the back of the wagon. She should climb inside, but she didn't know whether she could do it without help. A glance around showed Leo and Evangeline half-hidden from prying eyes as they stood near their wagon. Leo had one arm around Evangeline's waist, and she was saying something into his ear.

They were newlyweds, and their affection for each other was clear.

But as Felicity watched, Evangeline's much younger sister, Sara, darted past them. She headed beyond the wagon, straight for Leo's horse and its dangerous hooves.

Leo broke away from Evangeline. In two long strides, he whisked the girl into his arms. Just before the horse shied and stomped.

Holding the little girl, he turned back to his wife, but a memory trickled through Felicity's mind, overshadowing the present.

She'd been eight. It was late in the evening, and she'd been ironing one of her father's shirts for church the next morning. She hadn't realized her younger stepsister was awake until the sneaky girl had reached for the iron.

Norah had barely touched the hot surface when Felicity had shoved her away. She'd fallen to the floor, already sobbing, when Celia, her stepmother, had stormed over.

Felicity had opened her mouth, ready to explain that she'd saved Norah from putting her whole palm on the iron's surface, but she hadn't gotten one word out before Celia slapped her across the face.

She'd gaped at Celia, tears springing up, cheek stinging, as the woman had knelt over her crying daughter and soothed her with kind words.

A sharp hiss broke Felicity out of the memory as Leo poured water over the remains of the fire, dousing it until steam billowed. Evangeline was squatting next to Sara, packing up a crate near the wagon.

Felicity blinked away the memory, but her chest remained tight. She gripped the wagon sideboard, aching from that old hurt. She'd come so far, made her own way. She wanted a new home in Oregon, a home of her choosing, so badly that she trembled.

Abigail might think that God would provide for them, but Felicity knew it was the work of her own hands that had brought her this far.

She would figure out a way to get more food.

It was going to be up to her.

Chapter Two

"We drive up the bluff and then lower each wagon, with ropes, down the other side," said Hollis.

August exchanged a look with Owen, who sat next to him at the wagon master's campfire.

"There's been a rockslide," August said, repeating what he'd already told Hollis. "It looks like it happened weeks ago, but it washed out the bluff. We'll need to travel about a half mile west and then lower the wagons."

The fire was dying, and if they wanted to make twelve miles today, the wagons would need to move out within the hour. Scents of breakfast permeated the air as folks were slowly getting ready for the day.

Hollis consulted the small leather-bound book open on his lap. One dark-skinned finger tapped against the open pages. August had seen Hollis read from it before and knew it contained notes from the two overland journeys Hollis had undertaken before this one.

This time when Hollis looked up, his dark brown

eyes were more clear, though he squinted slightly in pain. "That'll put us close to the river drop-off."

August nodded. The narrow area where they could safely cross the bluff was dangerous, to be sure.

"We can drive as slowly as we need," Owen offered.

"And have the women and children walk ahead of the wagons," August added.

Hollis frowned but seemed to consider their advice. Finally, he sighed and rubbed the bridge of his nose. "We don't have much choice, do we?"

Owen was born a leader. He was confident, with a no-nonsense manner, and today August was glad for his steady presence. "Leo and Collin can lead the company up the hill," Owen said. "Once they are over, they can help each wagon tie off and make the descent."

It was a solid plan. August and Owen had talked it out for a half hour after August had ridden out early this morning, scouting the route ahead, before bringing the plan to Hollis.

It had become their routine as Owen had settled into the position of right-hand man for the injured wagon master. Hollis didn't have the stamina for a long, over-drawn meeting where they discussed pros and cons of what they should do going forward.

Hollis knew this land, knew the best routes and the dangers, but he couldn't sit a horse right now, which meant he couldn't judge the route for himself.

Owen and August had traveled on horseback from the gold fields in California to New Jersey, where they'd tracked down their half-siblings. August didn't know this terrain exactly, but on their journey East, he and Owen had faced raging rivers and wastelands and used their wits and instincts to make the journey. Everything they'd experienced had made August cognizant of the myriad of dangers out here in the wilderness.

Hollis had asked advice of the Mason brothers before his injury, expressed concerns to Owen as one of his captains in the company. Now it was Owen tasked with taking the wagon train through the next leg of the journey.

Hollis had to heal. August didn't want to think about what would happen if the man didn't recover. There was no one else qualified to lead these city people to Oregon.

Owen was a strong leader, but without a wagon master, it could mean disaster.

Abigail appeared from around Hollis's wagon. The woman was Hollis's self-appointed caretaker, and though August had never seen her without a smile, she was outright bossy when it came to the wagon master.

"You need to rest," she chided now.

Owen glanced at August, maybe in an attempt to give Hollis some privacy?

Hollis frowned. But it was easy to see the lines of pain around his eyes and mouth.

"I might sit in the wagon seat today," Hollis said with a stubborn twist of his lips.

"You'll do no such thing."

Owen tipped his head, indicating to August that it was time for them to leave.

August scrambled up from where he'd sat by the fire. He and Owen backed away before the young woman could turn her gaze on them.

"He didn't give approval," August said in low tones as

they returned to their wagon. Hollis had listened to their plan, but they'd been interrupted before he could agree.

Leo and Evangeline were nowhere to be seen, and August spotted Alice toting a washtub down toward the nearby creek. The Spencer family camp was empty and neat.

"He gave enough," Owen murmured. "Besides, our other choice is to travel five miles out of the way."

August vacillated. Maybe they *should* take the detour. It was safer, flatter ground.

"You mind saddling my horse?" Owen asked. "I need to check on the Earlywine family." He was gone before August had a chance to answer.

August rubbed the back of his neck, idly wondering if Alice had any coffee left in that pot on the tailgate of her wagon.

"You ever get tired of lickin' his boots?"

The gruff male voice came from what August had thought was a bundle of blankets near Alice's wagon. It was, in fact, a bedroll. Now Coop's sleepy head poked out of it.

August frowned. "What?"

"Seems like your brother sure does like telling you what to do. You ever get tired of following his commands like a lap dog?"

August bristled. He immediately thought that Coop needed a good walloping.

"Owen has to watch out for the entire company," he said.

"Seems like he don't boss ever'body else around the way he does you."

An old memory surfaced. He'd been all of thirteen,

16

and Owen had met him on the road as August was coming home from school. "Think it's about time you stopped attending school and started helping around here."

August had been disappointed but had agreed without question. By that time, he'd followed all of Owen's orders without question. Owen knew better. They'd both learned that the hard way.

"Stirring up trouble?" Owen asked Coop, joining them again. "Why don't you get out of that bedroll and help your sister pack up?"

Coop scowled.

Owen didn't seem to register it. He tipped his head and August followed him out of the circle of wagons and to the horses picketed nearby.

"The Earlywines weren't with their wagon. Must've gone down to wash up at the creek."

When August headed for Owen's horse, hefting the saddle to his shoulder, Owen paused on his way to fetch the oxen.

"You haven't forgotten our deal, have you?" Owen asked.

The change in subject threw August for a moment. When his mind finally caught up, he frowned. *The deal.*

Owen expected him to find a wife before they reached Oregon.

"Have you set your eye on anybody? We'll have Sunday service in a few days. Maybe you could ask a young lady to go walking."

What young lady?

August had barely wrapped his mind around the deal they'd struck days ago. Owen had promised to sign over the deed to Pa's homestead to August if he married before they reached Oregon. There were several young women in the wagon train, but August had been so busy with extra scouting duties and talking about the route with Hollis that he hadn't even had time to consider it. He told his brother as much.

Owen frowned. "You aren't going to renege, are you?"

August shook his head and tipped the saddle blanket over the horse's back. "I can't just choose a wife like drawing straws. But I haven't changed my mind."

Owen studied him for a long moment. "I just want you to be happy, you know." He clapped a hand on August's shoulder.

"I am happy," August said.

"Good." Apparently satisfied, Owen went to bring the oxen to the wagon to be hitched up.

August's thoughts rolled around the inside of his head like marbles. Owen thought he needed a wife to be happy, but August hadn't thought there was any particular rush. Yet he hadn't argued with his brother in years.

You ever get tired of lickin' his boots? Coop's rude question rattled in his mind.

Owen didn't push August around. They both knew Owen had the better head on his shoulders, and August couldn't bear to have any more blood on his hands.

He *did* want to get married.

And if Owen signed over the homestead, August would have what he'd always wanted. That, plus a wife.

* * *

18

By mid-afternoon, only half of the wagons had made it down the twenty-foot drop.

Felicity sat with Abigail in the shade of their wagon, watching and waiting as men lashed ropes to the wagons at the top of the cliff face and lowered them hand over hand down to the bottom.

It was slow work, heavy and difficult.

And it was dangerous.

She'd seen one man slip and nearly be pulled off the edge of the cliff. Rocks and dirt had knocked loose before he'd caught himself.

A fall like that would seriously injure a body.

Much worse if the wagon came down on top of that body.

When the next wagon was hanging from the cliff, still ten feet in the air, someone lost hold of one of the ropes. It rotated in midair, hitting the cliff face with one wheel and knocking loose soil and debris.

Felicity felt as if her heart might stop. She had no memory of the tornado picking up her wagon or hurling it through the air, but she couldn't breathe for remembering waking up buried underneath twisted and broken pieces of wood and metal.

She stood up painfully. When Abigail looked curiously at her, she motioned to the river and mimed walking.

"You're going for a walk? You want company?" Abigail was leaning on her elbows in the soft, long prairie grasses. She looked plum tuckered out. A moment ago had seemed only seconds from nodding off.

Felicity shook her head.

"Be careful," Abigail warned.

On this side of the bluff, vegetation flanked the river on both sides. It was cool and quiet along the bank, and the sounds of rushing water drowned out the distant cries of the men calling instructions to each other.

A dragonfly flitted across the expanse, momentarily skating on the water's surface before flying away. It was peaceful, and should've made her feel serene, but her mind flitted about like that dragonfly, reminding her that she and Abigail wouldn't have enough supplies to last them the journey to the Willamette Valley.

Birds chirped somewhere nearby. She didn't have a solution and she kicked at the ground, only for something to come loose and take a tumble. She glanced down, expecting a rock or small piece of driftwood.

But it wasn't a rock.

It was a chipped teacup.

How had it gotten down here?

At the muddy shoreline, she spotted a part of a wagon wheel. And that long metal piece might've at one time been an axle. Whatever else had once been a part of that wagon had long since washed away. Had a former pioneer attempted to pass the drop off by fording the river? Or perhaps they'd crashed off the cliff entirely and their wagon had been swept away.

The pieces of wagon that were left offered her no answers, so she kept walking.

She spied a single shoe on a sandbar thirty feet out into the center of the river and more debris the longer she followed the river.

She'd seen many discarded items on this journey, most of them in the first two weeks outside of Independence. It had happened in Hollis's wagon train, too.

Travelers realized that their oxen and horses were wearing out too quickly trying to pull the weight of belongings that were more luxury than necessity.

But this seemed different, somehow. More like her wagon that had been destroyed and left behind.

It made her sad.

Until the idea slipped into her mind.

What if she could find some items of value among this wreckage? And what if there was more to be found along the path they'd follow all the way to the Willamette?

Perhaps she could scavenge items to sell to or trade with soldiers in the fort. Or valuable items they could sell once they reached Oregon.

She didn't know whether or not it would work, but the idea gave her hope.

She began scouring the bank of the rippling, churning river. She picked up part of a crate—then discarded it almost as quickly as it fell apart in her hands.

Her heart leaped as she spotted a flash of some sort of fabric. Was it a dress? Or a man's shirt?

She had to pull it from the mud that had washed up and covered it almost entirely.

It wasn't clothing at all. It was a fancy lace tablecloth. Or had once been. She pushed it out into the water while holding to one edge, letting the stream wash away some of the mud.

She'd never seen anything so fancy.

The person who'd left this behind must have come from a wealthy family. No one on their wagon train would need something like this. Nor would any of the soldiers. But maybe there was someone already in

Oregon who would like a fancy decoration for their table.

She picked it up and attempted to wring it out. The movement wrenched her ribs, and for a moment she had to breathe through the pain. During her recovery, she'd learned to focus her stare on something distant, and she did so now.

Only as her breathing eased did she realize the brown thing jutting out from behind a white driftwood log several yards downstream wasn't a natural part of the landscape.

A satchel, she realized as she got closer. She knelt down and opened the flap to see what was inside. A fiddle. It looked a bit worse for wear, two strings broken and a piece chipped out of the face. Would it still be playable? She didn't know, but she took both the tablecloth and the satchel with her as she continued exploring downstream.

A shout from somewhere away from the river startled her and she realized just how long she'd been gone. Surely the rest of the wagons had been lowered down by now.

Felicity struggled up a small incline and found herself out on the prairie. Fear spiked for a moment before she caught sight of the wagons to the west of her position, as if they'd kept going without her.

Relief flowed through her. She tried not to tweak her side as she hurried toward the wagons coming into the final circle shape that meant they were going to make camp.

It was only when she'd reached the wagon and

Abigail had hurried off with a hasty, "There you are," that she realized no one had missed her.

If the wagons hadn't stopped for the night, would she have been able to catch up?

The sinking feeling in her stomach reminded her of when she'd been ten and had nearly been left at the schoolhouse after the community Christmas pageant. Her father and Celia had been loading the smaller children into the family wagon, bundling them with blankets. When Felicity had run up, panting and worried, Father had barely glanced at her, and Celia had chided Felicity for not paying attention.

More than once, she'd had to walk home alone after school because Celia had fetched the younger children but forgotten Felicity.

Back then, she'd been swamped with this same feeling, the feeling that she hadn't mattered. To anybody.

It made her ache with loneliness.

She allowed herself to wallow in it for only a few moments before she firmed her lips and lifted her chin and set about laying out the lace tablecloth in the grass so it would dry. The fiddle she tucked inside the wagon bed. She'd have to see about cleaning it and fixing it up later.

"That's real pretty." The male voice startled her, and she whirled with one hand over her heart, grimacing when her ribs protested the quick movement.

August stood considering the tablecloth. When he glanced at her, concern pushed his brows together. "I just wanted to come by and check on you. Haven't gotten to see you in a few days. You all right?"

She wasn't. Not with injuries continuing to plague

her and memories she'd rather keep locked away pressing in.

But the fact that he'd asked, that he'd made the effort to seek her out, somehow made her feel the slightest bit less lonely.

"You need anything—?"

"August!" A male voice called out, interrupting his question. It came from somewhere across camp.

He grimaced slightly.

She knew people needed him, and it warmed her that he cared enough to check on her. She motioned him to go on. She didn't have words to tell him thank you for bringing her out of the dark place inside, so she gave him the only thing she could.

A smile.

And she vowed to find a way to pay him back for his kindness.

Chapter Three

Two days after the first sighting of the buffalo herd, all August wanted was a bath and his bedroll. The evening shadows were lengthening, and he'd been in the saddle since breakfast.

Hollis had signaled and the wagons had circled up over an hour ago, but August had kept riding so he could get the lay of the land for tomorrow's travel. He'd scouted north first, seen wolf tracks along a muddy creek bank, scared a deer from a copse of scraggly cedar trees before turning west and making a wide arc back to the river.

The buffalo had moved now, surging ahead and to the south of the wagon train. There were so many that it was a breathtaking sight. But he could imagine how dangerous those hooves would be. One animal was big enough to knock over a wagon. Certainly, they could trample a traveler. So he was worried about their continued proximity.

The slow wagons couldn't outrun the buffalo.

Hollis thought they could use a couple of riders to

drive the buffalo alongside or away if they got too close to the wagons, but just thinking of that made August afraid. Maybe the animals would move on their own.

August was so caught up in worries about the buffalo herd that he almost didn't see the woman standing at the river's edge. The river was wide and flat here, with a wide muddy band on either side. Vegetation was sparse next to the water's edge. It looked peaceful and harmless.

At first, he thought she was simply walking along the bank. He'd already nudged his mare to turn back to camp but then his gaze held on the pale blue dress as he saw her falter. He might've expected the stumble to send her to her knees. Instead, she wobbled and jerked.

He wheeled the mare, suddenly realizing she wasn't standing along the water's edge. No, she was caught calf-deep in the mud. He urged his horse into a lope, pulling up when the ground beneath him changed from grass to that sticky mud.

"You need help?" he called out. From this close, he recognized Felicity.

She waved her hand, but there was something frantic about the motion. He was yards away. Her back was to him, so he couldn't make out her face. She tried to twist, and wobbled again, but her feet never moved. She lost her balance, bent over in half, using one hand to catch herself against the ground.

He saw the wince in the shape of her body. It must've hurt. He knew about the broken ribs. Then she pulled her hand free of the mud. Her shoulders were shaking. Was she crying?

"I'm coming. Hang on."

His mare didn't like the mud and shied away. "All

right," he said, patting his horse's shoulder. He dismounted and removed his rope that was looped over the saddle, ready to be used. He quickly tied one end to the saddle horn and started toward Felicity, unrolling the rope as he went.

The river gurgled beside them, wide but still powerful in this spot.

Now that he was closing in on Felicity, he could hear the ragged exhalations of her breath. Too fast, too loud. She was on the verge of panic. He could feel it.

He watched her struggle to lift her foot again as he carefully and quickly moved through the squishy, clay-like substance.

Instead of freeing herself, Felicity seemed to sink another inch.

He'd read about quicksand before. Thought it was only in deserts. And maybe this wasn't quicksand at all, but the way it sucked at his feet, the way each step squelched, made him believe it must be something similar.

"Don't fight against it," he called to Felicity. "I'm almost there."

Now she could twist her head and see him. He caught a glimpse of the wildness of her eyes, the tears streaking her cheeks.

"The more you struggle and pull, the faster you will sink," he said.

Somehow, his words seemed to have a calming effect.

He kept his feet from sinking in by moving quickly, though the mud wanted to suck him under. He could feel it with each step.

How could he avoid getting stuck just like she was? That's why he had the rope, he told himself.

He was only two steps away when he realized his hasty plan of grabbing her around the waist wouldn't work. She had a couple of busted ribs. He could injure her further if he wasn't careful.

"I'm going to tie the rope around us both," he told her. "The horse will pull us right out."

She seemed to be holding her breath. He could see it as he took that last step toward her.

"That means I'm going to have to be close to you," he explained.

She nodded with a single loud exhale.

He moved in close enough for her breath to heat the exposed skin of his neck above his shirt collar. He quickly looped the rope around both of their backs, putting in a tight knot near his left armpit. The mud was already above the tops of his shoes.

"Hold onto me," he said. "I don't want to hurt you—"

She had her arms around his waist before he could finish his sentence. Fine, then.

He put his arms around her, locking his clasp around the middle of her back. She was trembling all over.

"Tell me if I hurt you," he said.

She leveled a look on him before he realized the absurdity of his words. She couldn't speak.

"Squeeze me or knock your head into me."

Her mouth moved, but he didn't catch the silent words.

He whistled to his horse, two short chirps.

The mare backed up a step.

The rope pulled taut.

Another step from the horse. August felt the tug of resistance.

Another.

It all happened in the same moment. The pull from the rope, his feet slipping free—he hadn't sunk nearly as deep as she had. She lurched a little. He tightened his arms around her, still trying not to exacerbate her injuries.

Her grip on him shifted as his feet came free of the mud. She was pressed even closer, her arms coming up behind his back.

He had a flash of memory of another river, one icy and rushing and dark. Another woman, his mother. She'd cried out—

Felicity's feet came out of the mud with a loud slurp. The noise pulled August out of the terrible memory.

He stumbled but managed to keep his feet. A quick whistle halted his mare's progress. He changed his hold on Felicity, the rope slipping down as he swept her into his arms.

Her face had gone pale, and he couldn't make out her expression from this angle. "You all right?"

She nodded, her head brushing his shoulder.

Another few steps and they reached the grassy area near his mare, where the ground was firm. He gently set her down and straightened. "We didn't bust another of your ribs, did we?"

It was easier to focus on her, to untie the rope binding them together, to visually take stock of her muddy dress and the pink blotches on her face that showed she'd been crying, than to return to his memory. He could still feel the breathless grief—

"How'd you get so far from camp?" he asked. The words emerged a little harshly.

She shrugged, more tears spilling over. She reached up to brush them away and left a muddy streak on her cheek.

"Everyone's probably looking for you." He tried to wipe the mud from her cheek with his shirt tail. She was watching him with those big blue eyes. For a moment, his breath got locked in his chest.

She was pretty. Real pretty.

The realization hit him like a smack.

He blinked and the moment was broken. Flustered, he took a step back and let his hand fall to his side.

What was that?

He boosted her onto the horse and stepped away to grab the reins near the horse's snout when he saw the silver sparkle of light playing off the river. The memory threatened to suck him under, grief still as piercing as the day it had happened crushed his chest until he felt as if he couldn't breathe—

And then his gaze caught on something else. Around the bend in the river, a white wagon canvas flapped in the breeze. He'd been so focused on Felicity that he hadn't seen it before now.

"Might be another wagon train," he said. But when he took a few steps to get a better look, he saw two more wagons sitting at odd angles and different lengths apart. No oxen, no movement. Why hadn't they circled up for the night?

The tiny hairs at the nape of his neck prickled and stood upright.

Something was wrong.

Bad wrong.

* * *

Rachel Duncan had been in purgatory for four days.

Four days of crashing fear, wondering and worrying whether the men who'd committed this atrocity would return.

Four days of being virtually alone in the wilderness. She'd been too frightened to return to the wagon after what had happened. She couldn't bear to see the body of her beloved husband, Evan. He had saved her at the cost of his own life.

Three days of near starvation—she wouldn't count the first twenty-four hours, since she'd still had some energy from the food she'd eaten before.

Four days spent trying to keep her brother Daniel alive.

Four days worrying about the baby.

Her arm curved around her belly where she lay tucked uncomfortably between two trees, not far from the bank of the river.

Only days ago, Evan had teased her about not being able to get his arms all the way around her when they'd embraced, not with her big belly between them. Evan had been excited and proud, ready to be a papa.

More ready than she was.

She was terrified. More so now, with Evan gone.

What was she going to do? She didn't want to die out here.

And Daniel.

If Daniel could recover, he could help her. She and

her brother had had a tumultuous relationship for years, but surely, he would help her.

She forced herself to sit up, her head spinning for long moments as her belly gnawed with hunger. Earlier, she'd laid down for a nap and only now realized it was later than she'd thought. Afternoon, maybe? The light played tricks with her senses.

The baby moved strongly inside her, a twist that was both welcome and painful. *Oh, Evan.*

She stood on shaking legs and picked up the rifle she kept close. Little good it did. She strained her ears, listening for any sounds out of the ordinary.

Nothing.

"Daniel?"

She had left her brother lying in a hollow in the ground nearby. The best she could do was keep them both hidden until Daniel healed enough for them to move. Maybe today?

She knelt over him. He was wrapped in a woolen blanket that she'd grabbed when she'd found him still alive, lying yards away from Evan's body—

She couldn't think about that. About the other bodies.

"Daniel?"

He didn't answer, and for a moment in the shadowy stillness, with only the pale side of his face exposed, she thought he'd gone and left her, too.

"Daniel." She brushed a finger over his cheek, and he jumped.

He turned his head, scowled at her. "Leave me alone."

I can't. She swallowed the first fiery retort that

wanted to escape. Made her voice gentle, the way she'd seen Mama do far too many times. "How are you feeling?"

"Go away." His growl sounded almost exactly like Pa's. Rachel forced herself to breathe and not flinch away from him. They were all each other had out here.

"Can I tend your leg? Can you get up?" *We can't stay out here forever.*

When the gunshots had started, she'd seen Daniel fall first, beside his wagon. Then Evan had shoved her into the wagon, pushed her forcibly beneath the false bottom inside. He'd been wild, his eyes fearful and his jaw clenched with determination. "I'll come for you when it's safe."

But he hadn't come. She'd been trapped in the dark, enclosed space, running out of air, while screams and gunshots reverberated from outside the wagon.

Then voices.

She'd felt the motion as someone had stepped on the wheel and then boosted himself into the wagon bed. She'd almost called out, thinking it was Evan. She couldn't say what had stayed the words in her mouth.

Whoever it was had rustled around inside the wagon for long minutes.

Tears had streamed down her face in the silent darkness. Then she'd heard the murmur of other male voices.

A single gunshot in the distance.

Then nothing.

She'd waited for a long time, an interminable time. Until the silence was deafening, and she could bear it no longer. It was difficult, from underneath, to lift the heavy planks that covered her. She'd been shaking, desperately afraid that whoever had been shooting would come back.

She'd found Evan's body not far from the wagon, facedown. She'd fallen to her hands and knees, rolled him over to see his sightless eyes—

Now she broke out of the memories with a gasp. She couldn't afford to disappear into her grief. The baby was counting on her. She didn't want to die out here.

"Leave me be," Daniel said, his voice resigned.

She couldn't. He'd been shot in the thigh and when she'd checked his wound this morning, she'd found it inflamed, ugly red blotches all around the bullet hole. He claimed his wound made it impossible to walk.

"I need to—" Something frightened her into silence. She turned her head slowly, searching for...

What had it been? A twig snapping? A movement, deeper in the woods? A splash in the gurgling river?

Her breaths came frantically. She brushed fallen leaves over Daniel's blanket, hoping to hide him from view. She was in danger, standing out here in the open. Should she hide? Run?

If someone was still out there, she was done for.

* * *

"I'm going to get in the saddle behind you," August told Felicity. "Something feels wrong, and there's not time to take you back to camp before it gets dark."

Her eyes looked worried, but she nodded.

He put his foot in the stirrup and swung into the saddle behind her, only taking a few seconds to settle the reins. His arm wasn't wrapped around her, exactly, but it was a near thing.

He nudged his mare into motion. They rounded the wide muddy swath—he made note to himself to tell Hollis and Owen that the wagons had to avoid this area—and approached the first of the wagons.

He slowed his mare to a walk. "Halloo!"

Felicity jumped.

He murmured, "Sorry."

He was breathing in deeply to shout again when he saw a man's boot and part of a pant leg extended beyond the wagon. The boot was at such an angle that he instinctively knew it wasn't someone lying down taking a nap.

He reined in his horse, slowing her even further.

His trapping instincts took over as he scanned the area. There were two wagons within shooting distance, one with a huge rip in its canvas, the flap that hung down fluttering in the last of the evening breeze. The river burbled behind and to the left, but here there was no noise of crickets chirping, no flutter of birds' wings.

It was almost eerie in the silence.

Felicity turned her head slightly, enough that he could read the question in her expression just from the side of her face.

"There," he said. He pointed to the wagon and the boot beyond it.

He felt more than heard the soft intake of her breath.

His hand reached down for his rifle as he guided his mare in a wide arc around the wagon. It could be a trap. As the prone man on the ground came into sight, August knew that whatever this was, it was ugly.

A rust-brown stain covered almost the entirety of the

man's previously white shirt. His skin was pasty, and his eyes stared sightless into the sky above.

Felicity must've registered that he was dead, too, because she turned her head the opposite direction, rearing back in a way that pressed her ear against August's collarbone.

August kept his hand on his gun. Did the rest of the wagons contain a scene like this? It was entirely possible that whoever had killed this man was still nearby.

"I have to go closer," he said quietly.

Felicity shook her head. He glanced down at her. She was still looking away, her eyes tightly closed, her face scrunched up in denial.

Compassion stirred. She shouldn't have to see such violence. If he had any choice, he would take her back to the company. But what if there was someone alive among these wagons? Or what if there was someone lying in wait for the next wagon train? He and Owen could be leading their company straight into danger.

He had no choice but to investigate further.

"We won't stay long," he told her. "I just need to see—"

He didn't know what he was going to say.

He'd edged his mare closer to the wagon. He now saw a crumpled form in skirts lying facedown. A few feet beyond her, the body of a small boy.

He loosened up on the reins to press one hand against the back of Felicity's head, forcing her face into his chest. "Don't look." His voice was rough.

He felt her trembling against him, the soft catch of her breath.

His own voice broke when he called out, "Anybody alive here? We can help."

Nothing but silence answered him.

He pushed past the wagon and its scene of death and rode to the next one. At first, he thought it was simply empty, but then he saw the man's body lying half-in and half-out of the back of the wagon, arms and head down, a stain of blood marking the wood of the wagon.

"Anybody here?" he called out again.

The sky was growing darker. It was difficult to see if there was danger hiding in the copse of trees at the river's edge. They couldn't stay out much longer, but something pressed him to keep going.

He guided the mare on to the next wagon. Movement from underneath the wagon box had him drawing his rifle from its scabbard.

A coyote loped off, disappearing into some scrub at the river's edge.

August couldn't see any visible bodies. He guided his mare in a big circle around the wagon. Felicity raised her head at last. She turned toward him, her lips moving. He dearly wished he could understand her.

He thought he could read the word *who* on her lips.

"Who would do this?" he asked. It must've been close enough, because she nodded once.

"I don't know," he said. "It had to be an ambush, the way the wagons are spread out."

He edged the mare closer to where that coyote had disappeared.

"There was a woman back there," he said quietly. "She was shot in the back. Probably running away from whoever was doing the shooting. Sure seems like murder."

If anything, Felicity trembled more violently. If she'd have been Alice, August would've pulled her into a hug.

But Felicity wasn't a relation. He barely knew her.

A pattern in a patch of mud near the brush distracted him. Straight lines, like something had been dragged over it. Broken branches framed where something—or someone might be hiding down by the riverbank.

"That might be a fresh track," he told Felicity. "It rained last night, which would've softened up the ground."

He scanned the horizon in all directions. Nothing moved. His instincts had reared up when he'd noticed the seemingly abandoned wagons, but now they were still. He didn't truly know whether the danger was past, but his gut was telling him to check that track.

"I'm going to check it out," he said.

He swung his leg over the horse and dismounted.

She was saying something in her silent way, but her lips were moving too fast, and it was getting too dark for him to understand.

"I can't—"

She pointed to herself and then pointed to him.

"You want to—"

She was already swinging her leg over the saddle. If he hadn't been quick, he wouldn't have caught her waist as she scrambled off the horse.

"Easy."

She was breathing hard, her hair was wisping around her face. She still had that streak of mud across her cheek, and it hit him again, like a streak of lightning in the sky, how beautiful she was.

It wasn't the time for such a thought. He pushed it away as he reached for his rifle.

"Don't get too close to the river," he said. "I don't know if there's more of that quicksand-mud around here."

She followed close behind him as he pushed back some low cedar branches and followed where he imagined that track went.

There was a dip in the ground and then a drop off where the hill fell away to the river bottom. An old tree had fallen, who knew how long ago, and half-blocked off the washed-out area.

A twig snapped, He went on high alert, putting out his arm to stop Felicity behind him. He drew the rifle up to point at the ground several feet ahead of him. It would only take a second to bring it into firing position.

Felicity must have been holding her breath, because all he could hear was his heart thrumming in his ears.

And then a soft noise, half between a sob and a cry of pain.

He scrambled down the rest of the drop off, eyes scanning the area.

The fallen log had blocked off a tiny washout in the earth and formed a sort of protective area. Wedged inside it was a little girl, her face streaked with mud and tears.

The moment she saw him, her eyes went wide with fear. She squeaked in alarm and backed away.

Chapter Four

A sudden keening noise startled Felicity, who'd been frozen since August had apparently sensed something and scrambled down the washout. She jumped and didn't know whether to stick close to August or run back for the horse. She hadn't been able to breathe since he'd come across the first wagon and she'd glimpsed the dead man's body.

"It's a little girl," August said.

It was *what?* Felicity started after August, holding up her skirt when the incline and a tree root threatened to topple her. Heart pounding, she met him at the bottom of the steep gully and immediately caught sight of the small child huddling behind the fallen log.

"We're here to help you." August had crouched low, making himself less threatening.

"G-go away," the child gurgled. "You're a b-bad man."

August shifted his glance to Felicity. Then back to the little girl.

"My name is August. This is my friend Felicity."

Some warmth sparked in her chest when he claimed her as a friend. Only a true friend would've come after her when she'd foolishly been stuck in that mud. She'd been desperately afraid when he'd called out, but she'd recognized his voice. She didn't know why, but he'd come for her and helped her.

Having August near now made her the slightest bit less fearful.

"We're from another wagon train. Traveling west."

He was trying to calm the girl, who was shaking and sobbing softly.

"You need help," August said as he reached for her.

The girl shrieked, and Felicity fought the urge to cover her ears.

August stalled where he'd shifted slightly toward the fallen log and the girl.

"G-get away," the girl cried. "I want my pa!"

August scooted back and glanced between the girl and Felicity. Was he thinking the same thing she was? There'd been no sign of life in any of the wagons they'd come to. The other wagons beyond where August had followed this track were still and quiet, too. Surely if someone had been alive, they would've made some effort to move the wagons.

Then she realized she hadn't seen any animals in the haphazard wagon train. No oxen. No horses. No dogs barking.

What had happened here?

"We can take you to get some help. When's the last time you ate?" August tried once more, his words gentle. How did he stay so calm?

The girl shook her head. She was biting her lip, a

stripe of whiteness in the near-dark. She edged backwards, winced.

For the first time, Felicity noticed the angle of her leg protruding from behind the log. Felicity took two steps. They brought her to August's shoulder. She touched him, then pointed to the girl's leg.

Broken. It had to be.

August stood and pulled Felicity a few feet away. He seemed to be more confident that there wasn't danger nearby now because he'd lowered his rifle.

She'd seen him wear a serious expression like this once before—when she'd woken from unconsciousness after the twister had pinned her beneath the wagon.

"It's falling dark, and we can't leave her here," he said. "There's not time to go back to that wagon and make a torch. Will you help me?"

She nodded. She hadn't realized until he squeezed her hand that he'd even taken it. For such a tall, broad man, he was gentle.

He tugged her along with him, and they approached the girl together.

"We're going to help you," August said.

"No!" The girl tried to scramble back away from them, crying out when her leg dragged.

August kept his calm demeanor, though Felicity couldn't help noting the tremble in his hand.

"There's no one up there in the camp." He moved a branch out of the way and crouched in front of her. "We're gonna take you to our company, so we can get your leg fixed up."

The girl seemed to calm a bit, snuffling through her tears.

"What's your name?" August asked gently.

"Ben."

Ben. A boy's name?

He moved another branch, handing it off to Felicity, who put it out of the way. "That's an interesting name. Is it a nickname?"

She nodded, her breaths jagged.

"What is Ben short for?"

"Buena." The girl's voice wobbled.

"That's real pretty." A pause. "You ready? I'm gonna touch your leg now."

She cried out when he barely touched her foot.

To Felicity, he murmured, "It's swollen so bad, I don't think we can get the boot off. She's been like this for awhile—maybe several days."

Felicity's heart went out to Ben. She must have been terrified, out here alone with a broken leg that meant she couldn't get around. What had she witnessed?

She mimed eating with a spoon to August, whose eyes lit up with understanding.

"We've got some food back at our camp," August said. "Lots of it."

Ben seemed to consider that.

"Felicity must be an awful good cook. Her food always smells amazing."

She glanced at him, but his full attention was on Ben. She hadn't cooked anything since the twister had blown through. Had August really walked past her cookfire and noticed her food?

"She's real quiet since she got hurt in a bad storm."

Ben didn't complain when August edged her out of underneath the fallen log.

"But she's real good at helping get camp packed up."

Felicity didn't have time to bask in his praise because he glanced back at her. "I don't think we can put her on the horse without splinting the leg. Can you find a straight stick? Or piece of branch? It needs to be thick enough it won't break."

She didn't want to walk away from him, but the faster he got the girl's leg splinted, the faster they could return to the wagon train.

She rustled through the nearby underbrush, jumping when something cracked. It was August, shifting to kneel by Ben.

Felicity found two sticks that might work and quickly returned to him. She could barely make out his features in the dim light, but his eyes seemed warm.

He braced the leg and used some twine that he must've had on his person to splint the leg.

"We'll get you doctored up real good when we get back to our folks," he told Ben. "You ready? I'm gonna lift you up, all right? We'll go get that food."

Ben started crying again when he gently lifted her into his arms and straightened.

He looked to Felicity. "Can you follow me up the hill?"

She didn't have much choice, did she? The sky had darkened almost completely, and every tree cast a shadow that seemed ominous, as if they would stretch out their arms and grab her.

August started talking, weaving a story that Felicity vaguely recognized as a fairy tale she'd heard as a child. He kept talking as he boosted Felicity into the saddle with one hand. Her ribs panged, now aching with a fire that felt like a coal beneath her skin. She did her best to ignore it as he handed Ben up to her. He settled the girl across Felicity's lap, resting the splinted leg against the side of the saddle and tying it off.

Felicity was wondering how the horse would handle three passengers, even if one was as tiny as Ben, but August simply took the reins and began to walk. He'd only gone two steps when Ben broke into shuddering, deep sobs again.

"I want my pa! I want pa!"

August moved close. One hand rested on Felicity's knee. "I promise I'll come back and find him."

Ben quieted.

Even Felicity was comforted by the steady promise in his voice. She was thrown back to those terror-filled moments when she'd come to consciousness after the wagon had toppled on her.

He'd smiled at her and promised to get her out, promised to get her back to camp.

She'd believed him.

And he'd followed through.

She brushed her hand across Ben's forehead. Between her touch and August's promise, the girl calmed.

August went back to telling his fairy tale as he led the horse away with the reins. He moved faster than she expected, jogging through the night.

How did he even know which direction to go? The moon wasn't up yet, only a sky full of stars sparkling above them. But Felicity wasn't afraid. August would get them home safely.

August seemed larger than life, like a character from

a storybook. A woodsman who would never get lost, could solve any problem.

Sometimes she couldn't stop herself from watching him stride through camp. He was always on a mission. He scouted their path for the day. He'd rescued her and several others and been responsible for finding Hollis when he'd been injured and separated from the company.

And all of this with a calm, steady presence that made others admire him and want to follow.

She admired him, too. She couldn't seem to help it.

Hours later, August lifted his torch, the dancing light shifting and illuminating another prone body.

"Another one?" Collin asked.

Collin was a few months older than August and had a good head on his shoulders. Unlike Coop, who was a hothead and a wildcard and had been mixed up with some unsavory folks on this wagon train already.

"How many does that make?" Collin asked, voice subdued.

All August could do was shrug. Speaking the words felt too raw. Twenty-two travelers murdered in cold blood. Some of them children, though this small wagon train seemed to be made up of older couples or childless couples, for the most part.

Who could do such an evil thing? He couldn't fathom it.

"All the food supplies are gone from this wagon, too."

Collin rode close, holding his torch in a way where he could see inside.

"It had to be some kind of raid," August said. "We haven't seen one animal dead from a gunshot." In fact, they hadn't seen any oxen or horses at all.

Hoofbeats pounded and a torch headed their way. Moments later, Leo reined in. "Any sign of life?"

August shook his head.

"I don't like it," Leo said. "There had to have been a war party or at least eight or nine men working together to take out an entire wagon train."

"The two wagons at the front tried to get away." August pointed over his shoulder at the two wagons farthest west. "They outpaced the rear wagons but one of them broke an axle trying to turn too sharply."

Leo's horse was agitated, snorting and high stepping as his half-brother kept his seat. He couldn't read Leo's expression in the flickering torchlight, but the horse was reading him fine. Leo must be worried about his wife and young ward back at camp. They'd left ten men stationed around their circled wagons, alert for any danger.

But Leo would want to protect his wife himself.

And August couldn't stop thinking about the little girl named Ben.

By the time he'd led Felicity and Ben into camp, there'd been several men with torches lit, ready to look for Felicity, who hadn't been seen since they circled up. Leo had been one of them. When he'd heard August's report of what he'd seen, he'd started calling for men to make up a search party and a guard.

In the midst of all of that, Ben had withdrawn, tucking her face into Felicity's shoulder. Felicity had cupped the back of her head in a motherly gesture. It had seemed to soothe the girl, but more than that, it had somehow pricked a reminder of August's own mother. She'd never shied away from affection, often setting her hand on top of August's head.

He could still feel the ghost of that touch, after all this time.

He'd promised Leo that he'd come back to lead the men to the site of the murders, then guided his horse through the wagons toward the tent that had been set up for Felicity and Abigail. Alice had met him there, having obviously overheard some of his conversation with Leo and the other captains. She was ready to help when August lifted Ben from the back of the horse.

"I sent for Maddie," Alice murmured as he handed over Ben.

"Good."

Maddie was their unofficial healer since there wasn't a doctor in the company. She could help set Ben's leg.

Felicity had already kicked her leg over the saddle when he moved back to help her off the horse. He was careful not to squeeze her waist tightly as he set her to the ground, aware of her previous injuries. In the bright fire-light from camp, he could see just how disheveled she was, her hair coming out of its braid and a scratch on her arm, her skirts inches deep in dried mud. He caught another glimpse of that streak across her cheek. Somehow that motherly touch he'd witnessed, and the sight of that silly mud, had muddled his thinking, because he caught himself raising his hand to wipe it away.

Her eyes held a question, and he grimaced because

there wasn't time to talk to her, make sure she was all right.

"No!" Ben was shrieking and flailing her arms at Alice, who'd set her on a pallet next to the fire, where Maddie would have a clear view of her injuries.

Felicity hung back while August squatted next to Ben. "Hey. Alice is just trying to help."

Ben snuffled and wailed, "I want my pa."

"I'm gonna go back and try to find him." The words tasted bitter in his mouth, because if there'd been anyone alive among those wagons, they would've answered when he called earlier.

"Maybe some food—" he turned to say the words to Alice, but Felicity was already there with a tin of beans and cornbread.

Ben fell on it, slurping and eating almost like a wild animal.

Alice watched with wide eyes.

He caught the wince from Felicity and the way she pressed one hand against her side.

"You need rest," he told her.

She answered him, silently, but her lips moved too quickly for him to make out any words.

He shook his head. Sighed. "We need a better way to communicate."

Leo called for him. He looked back at Felicity, who was making a shooing motion.

She wanted him to find the murderers. He wanted that, too. So he needed to go . But he had one more thing to say. "Thank you for helping with her. I'm not sure I could've gotten her back here without you."

"August," Leo snapped, and August realized he'd been lost in the memory, staring off into the darkness.

"Any tracks to indicate which direction the killers went?" Leo pressed. He seemed impatient. Had he already asked the question once before?

"Nothing," Collin said.

But Leo was watching August, waiting for him to speak.

"Remember that storm two days ago?"

Both men nodded, and August was struck by their similarities. "I think whatever happened here happened before that storm. If it was more recent, there'd be some kind of tracks."

"The bodies haven't been mauled by wildlife yet," Leo murmured.

"We need to bury them," Collin said.

"I'm more concerned about moving away from here quickly," Leo said. "What if whoever did this is still out there?"

August hadn't been able to shake the feeling of eyes on him all night. He told himself the awareness was simply because of the carnage they'd discovered and because it was dark.

"Our wagon train is five times bigger than this one was," Collin argued. "We'd take them out—"

"There's no guarantee of that," he interrupted quietly. "Whoever did this probably snuck up on the last wagon. They had a plan, and there had to have been a whole passel of them. We shouldn't risk any of our caravan."

"You're both right," Leo said grimly. "It's inhumane not to give these folks the burial they deserve. But we need to do it quickly and move on."

He could still hear the echo of Ben's voice in his head. Was one of these unfortunate souls her father? She'd seemed to insist he was alive. But maybe she'd needed to hold on to that hope to stay alive.

"Let's start gathering up the bodies," Leo said. "Send someone back to the wagons to bring some shovels. The faster we get this done, the faster we move. Even if it means working all night."

Collin nodded and wheeled his horse to take the news to the other searchers.

"Mind if I take one more look around?" August asked. "Ben was insistent that her father was out here."

Leo glanced at the wagon nearby and the bodies on the ground beside it, then quickly away. "She was lucky you found her. You think there's enough luck to find her father alive?"

August shook his head. "I don't know. But I promised her I would try."

Leo nodded his permission. August started making slow circles around the wagons, gradually expanding his search radius. It'd only taken him a few seconds to notice the track in the mud from where Ben had dragged herself down that incline to hide.

There was no other sign of anything bigger than that coyote he'd seen.

Until he splashed through a tributary, a smaller creek branching off the river, and caught sight of a man's boot print on the muddy bank.

He had his hand on his rifle, ready to signal to the other men, when a deadly voice hissed, "Put your hands in the air."

Chapter Five

Rachel kept her body hidden behind the tree as much as she could. The baby she was carrying inside her made it more difficult. The heavy pistol had been her husband's and weighted her arm, but she had to protect herself. Had to protect Daniel. She didn't let her arm waver even when the man on horseback with the torch remained where he was.

"Go away." She made her voice as deep and menacing as she could.

The baby kicked violently, the movement inside her just as strange as it had been when it was a light flutter. This kick hit something tender underneath her right ribcage and she bit back a gasp.

"I'm from another wagon train. We're camped about a half mile down the river."

Her heart leaped, but she stamped down the beat of hope that filled her. She'd had hope before.

Two days ago, she'd been foraging for berries or edible roots and thought she'd heard a horse approach.

She'd been praying for help, desperate and hungry. But she'd hidden herself by lying in a small dip in the ground and covering herself with decaying leaves. It had smelled disgusting—she still hadn't rid herself of the stench. It was soaked into her hair.

It had been the right choice. Only moments later, she'd gotten a glimpse of the rider through her leafy cover. It had been one of the men who'd attacked the wagon train. Maybe even the man who'd shot and killed Evan.

She'd held her breath until he'd wandered away, but she hadn't slept since then. She couldn't trust this man, this stranger.

"I'm not gonna hurt you," he said.

He sure sounded sincere. The flickering torchlight illuminated his face, though his hat threw shadows across his eyes. He had a craggy look about him, broad-shouldered and big. His hair was of a medium darkness. Maybe chestnut brown, though she couldn't be sure in this light. She tried not to think about the fact that if he came off the horse and came at her, she would be done for.

The pistol she held had no bullets.

"My name is August Mason. I mean you no harm. My companions and I helped a little girl from your company. Ben."

Her heart twisted. Ben was alive? She didn't know the little girl well, only through the weeks of traveling together. But if it was true, did it mean this man was a friend and not a foe?

Her memory fractured and for a moment Rachel was reliving the terrible moments when she'd found

Glinda, her sister-in-law, lying on the ground. Dead. Simon had been caught up in his mother's arms. Dead, too.

Rachel felt the screams rising in her throat but fought them down. Tried to shake off the horrific memories.

"You could be lying," she said. "Maybe you're just pullin' my leg that you helped Ben."

"She told me her name," he said gently. "Her leg was broken, and she was real hungry—she's been hiding out here as long as you have."

Four days.

Four days of panicked fear, trying to figure out if the attackers had left any animal behind, any food, trying to keep Daniel alive.

Worrying about the baby, who hadn't moved inside her for the first terrifying hours after the attack.

Daniel moaned, the sound loud in the darkness.

She'd hidden him behind a fallen log and covered him with several branches, tried to make it look natural. He hadn't wanted anything to touch him, had been adamant and angry when she'd tried to explain why he needed to be hidden.

August's head turned toward the sound, ten feet from her position.

She leaned farther out from the tree, careful to keep her big belly hidden behind it.

"If you truly want to help us, you'll give us a horse. And some food."

Daniel needed help. She didn't know how to care for the wound in his leg. He'd gotten quieter today, was burning up with fever. But she still couldn't trust this stranger.

Another voice rang out, from further downstream. "August! What've you got?"

Alarm spiked. Was this a part of the group that had attacked them before?

"I can handle this," August called back.

How exactly was he planning to handle her?

She pointed the gun right at him, her hand clearly shaking now, but there wasn't anything she could do about that.

"Get outta here, mister. I'll shoot. I promise I will."

Daniel moaned again.

August looked conflicted. "I don't wanna leave you out here. Is there someone hurt? We've got a healer back at camp."

A healer.

Her breath caught again. Daniel needed more help than she could give. She'd tried to make a poultice with tree bark and mud, but without a pot to boil it in or fire to warm it, she'd given up. She'd been afraid to infect Daniel's wound.

She would also need a healer when the baby came. And that might not be much longer.

She didn't want to have her baby alone in the wilderness.

She wanted Evan.

Tears clogged her chest so suddenly that she couldn't push them back down, not fast enough. She hadn't let herself cry. Not through any of it. And now a sudden tear rolled down her cheek.

Something came crashing through the underbrush to her left.

"Owen, no—"

She swung around, pointing her empty gun at the horse and rider.

Too late.

The man rode his horse right toward her. When she stepped out of the way, he kicked out with his leg. She was too slow, thanks to her bulk, and he caught her shoulder with enough momentum that she spun and fell to the ground. She twisted at the last moment, her arms coming to surround her stomach as best she could.

The gun flew free, useless as it was.

She couldn't breathe, the air knocked from her lungs. "Owen!"

The man was already on top of her, pinning her shoulders painfully to the ground. Maybe he'd flown off his horse even as he passed her.

"Stop!" August shouted. He'd jumped off his horse too. The torch was closer, throwing flickering light that illuminated the bearded man too close.

"She's just scared!"

"She?" The man—Owen?—froze, though his hands still banded her wrists like manacles.

He glanced at her face with wide eyes, then his gaze traveled down to where her coat—Evan's coat—had fallen open, revealing the bulge of her belly.

He had to have felt it when he'd jumped on top of her, but maybe he hadn't realized.

He sat back, though he still had hold of her hands. "You're pregnant."

"Let me go."

"Let her go." August's calm demand came at the same time she hissed the command.

"She was pointing a gun at you." The man sounded angry still. Or maybe disgusted.

"She's frightened. She's been out here for days."

He finally released her. She scrambled backward, putting her back against the tree trunk. The baby moved strongly inside her, twisting so deeply that she gasped and pressed a hand against her belly.

August was wide-eyed, but Owen's eyes were still squinted suspiciously.

"Come to the wagon train with us," August said gently. "We've got more protection, and you can decide what to do from there."

He sounded reasonable. He'd walked over to the gun and picked it up. She wanted to shout at him before he opened the chamber, but a sudden sob overtook her and stole her voice. He showed the empty chamber to Owen, who stood up and extended his hand to her.

"Who else you got out here with you?" Owen's voice was far more gruff than August's.

She ignored his demanded question and pushed herself to her feet without taking his hand. She didn't need his help. And even if she did, she would never accept his.

Chapter Six

From inside her tent, Felicity heard the murmurs as camp came to life. It sounded as if a group of men was going over to the site of the attack to dig a large grave. Several women's voices chimed in, too. The other travelers must want to see if there were any salvageable supplies in the wagons, too.

Felicity slipped out of the canvas tent as the sun broke over the horizon. The sky was streaked with soft pinks and oranges, but she was more focused on the group of people disbanding from around a campfire several yards away.

Her stomach was growling for sustenance, and she felt bleary and achy all over.

Abigail stooped over a cookfire much closer—it was amazing how sound traveled out under the open sky— and as Felicity approached her, Leo and Owen made their way between two wagons and straight toward Abigail.

Abigail glanced up at Felicity's approach. "Good morning."

Felicity pulled a face. It wasn't a good morning.

Not after the night she'd had last night.

Abigail shared a commiserating glance. "It was a long night, wasn't it? Here. This'll help." She lifted a tin mug of coffee.

Felicity glanced over her shoulder to where Maddie and Lily Fairfax had been emptying a crate near their wagon. She'd heard them talking about visiting the wreckage of the other wagons. Were they planning to look for supplies?

She gulped the coffee, aware that Leo and Owen were closing in on their cookfire.

"What do you mean, a long night?" Owen asked as he came to stand opposite them.

Abigail stirred the skillet of frying potatoes and ham. "The little girl woke several times. She was disoriented and upset. I tried to speak to her, but she seemed to only want Felicity."

Felicity holding the little girl on her lap had been the only thing that seemed to calm the child.

Five times.

Her broken sleep was the reason she felt as if she was sleepwalking this morning. Everything seemed fuzzy and a little distant. Except for her desire to go to the broken wagons and see if she could find anything of value. She and Abigail needed money. And it was easier to focus on that than the remembrance of comforting Ben.

Those moments in the dark of night had reminded her of a time when she'd been all of ten. Her stepsister Angela had been suffering with a terrible fever. Papa had been working long hours in the mines and sleeping like the dead when he was home. Celia had been caring for her newborn, Scott, who was only three weeks old.

Celia had insisted Angela could sleep through the night, even though her bright pink cheeks and dull eyes showed the fever ravaging her.

It was Felicity who had taken pity on the little girl who'd cried all night long. Felicity who had kept a bowl of water nearby to dampen the rag she laid over Angela's burning forehead. Felicity who had carried her about the small bedroom, swaying her back to sleep.

Angela's fever had broken near dawn. Celia had claimed exhaustion and demanded Felicity make breakfast for her and the two older children.

Comforting Ben in the night had brought back those conflicting feelings from Felicity's childhood. She'd dearly loved her little sister. The tot had a habit of following Felicity around as she did chores, trying to copy everything she did.

But there was a part of Felicity that resented her sister. All her half-siblings, actually. If she hadn't been caring for Angela, Felicity would've slept through the night and been fresh when she needed to make breakfast and help her siblings dress for school. Instead, she'd fallen asleep over her slate that afternoon and received a rap on the knuckles from her teacher.

Punished, because she was exhausted from caring for her little sister.

Felicity started as she realized Maddie and Lily were leaving the circle of wagons. She set the coffee cup on the ground near Abigail, shooting her friend an apologetic look for leaving the dirty dish.

She was taking the first step away from the fire when Leo held out his arm, "You goin' somewhere?"

She pointed to where Maddie and Lily had just disappeared, hating that her voice didn't work. She didn't want to fall behind.

"Can it wait a moment?" Owen asked.

When the captain asked, it wasn't really a question. Owen had a commanding presence about him that made it difficult to say no. Though this morning, he looked as tired as she felt.

She started to shake her head, but Leo was already talking.

"Several men are digging graves this morning. We don't dare stay for long, not when we don't know if whoever attacked those wagons is still out there."

Owen nodded. "We've talked with Hollis. We'll take the survivors with us to the next fort."

Leo looked grave. "Ben will need someone to look after her, with that leg and being so young."

"Of course, she'll stay with us," Abigail said easily.

No! Felicity's lips formed the word but, of course, no sound emerged. She shook her head. Abigail looked at her askance.

"The two of you and Hollis have done a lot for Felicity and me," Abigail said. "You helped us when the storm robbed us of our wagon and supplies, so if you need our help caring for Ben, you've got it."

Felicity trembled with the desire to refuse. But with every word Abigail said, she realized just how callous that would prove her to be.

She and Abigail wouldn't be here now if August and his brothers hadn't helped them. She didn't like to think about what would've become of them if they'd been left at that fort with no money and no transportation. No friends.

But she'd left home at sixteen for a reason. She'd had her fill of taking care of children. She certainly felt compassion for Ben. The little girl had been through something traumatic. There'd been no word of her father being found. And she was injured. But Felicity didn't have to be the one to help her.

Abigail had been so busy caring for Hollis. Felicity wasn't supposed to know the wagon master had a severe concussion and that he couldn't sit a horse because of it. Abigail had nursed him for days and would likely continue—he'd shouted everyone else out of his wagon.

Which meant the burden of watching over Ben would fall to Felicity.

Owen was watching her with narrowed eyes. She felt like he could see inside her—see too much.

She didn't like it.

She cast her eyes down.

At that moment, a wail came from inside the tent. A sound so mournful that Felicity's heart panged.

August crossed between two wagons, carrying something in his hands. He set it down on a barrel near the wagon he shared with his brother and made for the tent.

Felicity had left the flap partially open. He ducked inside easily, murmuring something she couldn't hear from this distance.

Ben quieted.

When August emerged from the tent, he held Ben in his arms. She took her bearings and then pointed a small arm directly at Felicity. Whose stomach twisted.

She didn't want this.

But she felt the weight of Leo and Owen's expectations as they watched this unfolding. Abigail, too, believed Felicity was a kindhearted person who would want to help.

"Morning," August said easily.

Ben held out both arms toward Felicity, but August shook his head. "Felicity's ribs hurt, remember? She can't hold you like I can. But we can eat breakfast right here next to her, huh?"

Felicity sat down on an overturned crate and August dragged another close. He settled Ben on his knee, careful of her splinted and wrapped leg.

August's biceps brushed against Felicity's shoulder. Ben tipped her head so that it leaned on Felicity's shoulder. She burrowed her face into Felicity's neck.

August was close, and he shared a compassionate glance.

Something in Felicity's heart shifted. They were right, of course. Ben needed help. And Felicity would give it. Until the fort.

But she wouldn't forget about her mission in the meantime.

* * *

August hadn't slept for what felt like days.

He strode into camp mid-morning, after tying off his horse to the wagon. Weariness demanded he rest his eyes for a bit, but there was far too much to do.

He was distracted by the sight of the very pregnant woman who'd ridden back to camp with him last night.

She had one hand pressed to the bottom of her belly and was pacing back and forth outside a tent where Maddie had doctored the man with the gunshot wound—the pregnant woman's brother.

When she stopped pacing and started toward him, August's feet took him in that direction without conscious thought. The woman looked him straight in the eye. She looked as weary as he felt. Purple circles under her eyes and the droop of her shoulders revealed how little she'd slept. The bottom of her skirt was caked in six inches of mud.

He was still amazed she'd kept the both of them alive out there.

"I'm Rachel," she said.

"August."

"I wanted to say thank you for helping me and my brother, Daniel, last night."

He nodded. Couldn't keep his eyes from darting to her belly and back up to her face. "You all right?" He'd tried to warn Owen—his gut had been screaming a warning that she wasn't going to shoot anybody with that revolver. And when he'd seen Owen take her crashing to the ground, his heart had leaped into his throat.

He hadn't known she was pregnant then. Not until his torch had revealed her body.

Now her mouth twisted. "No thanks to that varmint who tackled me." She still sounded angry, her eyes flashing with it.

"That's my brother. Owen."

He saw the flush slip into her cheeks, the chagrin in her expression.

"It's all right," he said quickly. "He's one of the captains of our company. A good leader."

He was trying to explain why Owen had been protecting him, why she might trust him, but with every word he said, her frown only grew. He knew his brother's style of leadership wasn't for everyone. But Owen had protected the folks out here plenty of times.

"How's your brother?" he asked, changing the subject.

She glanced over her shoulder toward the tent, bit her lip. "Maddie—was that her name?"

He nodded.

"She said there's an infection. Gave him some tea and put new bandages on his wound." She hesitated, as if there was more she wanted to say. But then she shook her head and smiled slightly at him. "I don't suppose you know how we might find transportation to take us back East?"

She wanted to go back?

She must have seen the skepticism in his expression. Her smile tilted. "Moving to Oregon was my husband's idea." Now there was definitely something behind her words. "He's..." Her breath stuttered. "He's gone now. So are my sister-in-law and my nephew. There's nothing in the West for me."

Compassion stirred. She'd lost her husband and loved ones. She wasn't thinking straight, wasn't in any state to make a big decision like this. But she didn't have much choice, did she? Not with that little one on the way.

"I can ask around," he said. "I'm not sure anyone will be willing to part with a wagon."

And it'd be dangerous for her and that brother to travel alone. Real dangerous.

"Thank you. Even a... even a horse could work."

He hesitated, but asked, "Can you tell me what happened?"

Owen had been busy locating bodies and overseeing the digging of a big grave. He'd want to know, and August could be the intermediary since Rachel didn't seem as if she'd been seeking his brother out to pass along information.

She crossed her arms, wrapping them around her as best she could. Her eyes went far off. "Gunshots came out of nowhere. Men on horses, wearing bandanas covering their faces. Evan—my husband tried to outrun them, but the wagon was too slow. He returned fire."

Her voice broke and she brushed her cheek with her hand. "I saw my brother go down." Now her words came faster, falling one right after the other, as if she needed to be finished. "Evan pushed me inside the false bottom of our wagon. He hid me away. When I emerged, Evan was dead. And everyone else. Daniel was still breathing, but he wouldn't speak to me. I dragged him down by the river so we'd be out of sight."

They were strangers to each other, but he couldn't help himself. He reached out and put his hand on her arm. Her fingers curled over his hand as he felt the trembling breath she took. How was she holding herself together?

"I'll help however I can," he said.

"Thank you."

He saw the sparkle of tears in her eyes before a

female voice called out for her. Maddie, standing outside the tent. "He's asking for you."

Rachel excused herself, and he was left staring after her. She was in a difficult situation, to be sure. When he turned around, thinking to see if Alice had any coffee brewing, he saw Ben and Felicity sitting by the fire. He went to join them.

He squatted next to Ben. "How are you feeling? Maddie been by to doctor your leg yet?" He could see the answer. She still wore the hasty splint he'd made. Daniel's wound must be bad.

"I want my pa." Ben's lower lip quivered.

"I know, kid."

He glanced over to Felicity. "How are you?"

She shrugged, and he realized in all the busyness of the morning that he'd forgotten to give her the item he'd found. He straightened and jogged over to his wagon, where he'd sat the slate on the tailgate. He brought it back to Felicity. Her forehead wrinkled in confusion.

"I traded the Smith family for it." He handed it to her. She stared at the flat, dark-gray board. He handed her the chalk, only a part of a piece. Maybe he'd find more at the next fort.

She bent her head as the chalk scritched on the surface. Ben seemed distracted, dipping a long stick in and out of the fire. He sat down on the log next to Ben.

When Felicity was finished writing, she tipped the slate so he could see it.

Thank you. When she looked up, she was beaming.

Seeing her smile was like getting kicked in the stomach. He'd thought her pretty—was it only last night?—but when she smiled like that, she was beautiful.

He found himself smiling in response. "I'll ask again. How are you this morning?"

She wrote on the slate again. *Couldn't sleep.*

"Sore?"

Ben woke often.

Ah. That made sense, because of her injury and being away from the people she loved. He hated that he hadn't been able to locate her father.

He felt an urgency to go back out and resume his search. His exhaustion hadn't faded any, but Ben needed her pa. Or needed to know what had happened to him.

Ben scooted closer and leaned her head on his shoulder. "Will you stay with me tonight?"

Something hot lodged in his throat. "I can't stay in your tent, kid."

Ben drooped.

"Why don't we eat breakfast together?" he suggested.

Ben lit up. And if he wasn't mistaken, Felicity blushed slightly, though her face was turned down toward the slate.

Ben sighed and tipped her head against his shoulder again.

When Felicity tilted the slate toward him, she'd written, *Thank you for helping her.* She wore a soft smile, not the beaming one he'd seen earlier.

But it still made him realize...

He'd do anything to see her smile.

Chapter Seven

"Hollis said we need to stay near the river."

August was shaking his head even before Owen finished the sentence. It was late afternoon and the two of them had taken a turn at digging the grave needed to bury thirteen bodies. Now they were headed to their wagon to eat some grub.

Hollis had called for the funeral in ninety minutes. They would pull up stakes in the morning and move on. August was itchy to be back on the trail.

"Those buffalo are scattered just to the west of us," August replied. "And they've stayed that way for the past week—except for the day they tracked north of us."

"We can't leave the river behind," Owen said stubbornly.

"Yes, we can. The quicker, the better."

A heaviness hung in the air, a feeling that seemed to permeate Hollis's wagon train, too. Most of the travelers felt the same way August did. He'd heard murmurs as he'd walked through camp. Folks were scared. They wanted to leave this cursed place.

Owen swept his hat off and ran his hand through his hair in frustration. "The oxen and horses need water. There's fish to supplement our food."

"What about the people who murdered all those folks?" August lowered his voice as they drew near to camp. He was glad to see the watch with their rifles was still patrolling outside the ring of wagons. It had put more work on the womenfolk, with the men split between the watch and digging graves for those unfortunate travelers, but that couldn't be helped.

"No matter which way we travel, we can't outrun them if they decide to come for us." August didn't like being vulnerable.

Owen knew the danger. Traveling with the company was much different than the travel they'd done on their way East. Two men on horses could travel much faster than these slow wagons and people walking.

"At least if we move away from the river, we might avoid the buffalo."

"Hollis doesn't think so."

"Hollis isn't in any condition—" He cut himself off as Owen lifted a hand to wave to the nearest guard. Leo. August glared at his brother and lowered his voice. "Hollis hasn't seen the buffalo for himself. He doesn't know the danger."

August had been impressed with how Hollis had protected the wagons and people thus far. But his notes from his two previous journeys had listed only a dozen, or perhaps thirty, buffalo. The herd that had been moving through this area must number in the thousands.

August had only been able to guess as it spread over the plains and out of sight.

Owen sighed. "I don't want to fight."

August didn't either. But it stung that his brother didn't trust August's judgment on this. Too much a reminder of August's past failings.

"Everything in order?" Leo asked as the brothers neared.

"As close as can be," Owen said.

His dismissal was clear.

August ground his back teeth but let his gaze roam as he moved to the back of his wagon. Alice was cooking something over the fire. His stomach growled. Stella and Collin sat on a pair of crates in front of the Fairfax wagon, their heads together bent over a book.

Felicity and Abigail were speaking in hushed tones.

Leo leaned around the wagon to speak to August. "How did it go last night? Find anything useful?"

August felt Owen bristle from feet away.

Leo had been on watch when August had left camp in the early hours of the morning. It was easier for August to watch the two women than to meet his brother's gaze. Felicity was scribbling on the slate, and he felt a small rush of gratification that he could help her communicate.

Abigail shook her head sharply and said something he couldn't hear.

"You went out again alone? Why?" There was a sharpness to Owen's voice.

Finally, he turned to face his brother. "I couldn't sleep."

Owen's eyes flashed. He was angry. "You could've been killed if someone was still out there."

"No one was out there."

It had been ghostly quiet, other than the usual night noises of singing crickets and a frog in the creek. August had searched high and low, spending hours through the night and early morning looking for any trace of another survivor. He couldn't stop thinking about Rachel, alone in the world except for her brother. Couldn't stop looking for Ben's father.

This morning, he'd taken her to where the corpses had been laid out side-by-side, wrapped in quilts or blankets, whatever could be found. They'd pulled back the blanket from each man's face. Ben had shaken her head every time.

Her father wasn't among the dead.

She'd cried quietly after the ordeal. He'd carried her back to camp and put her to bed in Abigail's wagon. She was probably still sleeping. And he was still riddled with guilt. August hadn't seen hide nor hair of any other survivor. And tomorrow morning, they were going to have to move on.

Leo excused himself and went over to say something to Alice. Coop appeared, crossing between two of the wagons to join the duo.

"You can't just ride out alone," Owen said, the frustration rolling off him. His commanding tone and arms crossed stance with feet spread wide made August feel prickly.

"I scout every day for Hollis."

"That isn't the same," Owen argued.

"What's different?"

"Everything," Owen burst out. "You said yourself that the brigands that murdered those folks might still be out there."

Owen was wrong. He was acting like a mother hen. But August understood, a little.

He clenched his teeth against the desire to press his case.

Owen stared at him, eyes slightly narrowed. "Alice made supper for us. Why don't you go get something to eat?"

He posed it as a question, but August heard the command behind it.

"I can wait," he said.

Owen leveled a look on him.

"Fine," he gave in with bad grace. He stomped over to Alice's fire, where Leo was snapping at Coop.

"I told you to take a turn with the digging."

Coop seemed almost lazy as he replied, "You did not."

Alice handed August a plate of food, shaking her head slightly.

A muscle jumped in Leo's cheek. "Yes, I did."

"Well, I musta misunderstood."

August turned away, though he didn't walk off. He should make sure Alice didn't need anything.

His shoulders felt tight. He rolled them as he chewed a bite. He usually got along with Owen. Was this tension between them only because of the circumstances? Or was a relationship like the one Leo and Coop had what he could expect with his brother in the future?

He didn't like thinking it.

He needed something to distract him.

Lacy Williams

* * *

I want to go search the wagons.

Abigail read the words Felicity had scrawled on the slate and glanced up with wrinkled brows. The two women had been to the creek to wash the dishes from an early supper. Now they were packing them away.

"What, the—" she nodded her head in the direction the men and some women had been going all morning. *"Wagons?* Whatever for?"

Felicity had already used the side of her hand to clear the slate. *Find supplies.*

Abigail shook her head. "It's a travesty, what happened. You shouldn't raid their wagons."

The people from the other wagon train were dead. They didn't need the supplies any longer. But Felicity hesitated over the now-blank slate. How did she explain that?

Abigail didn't need her to. "I know some of the others have been over there, but it's not right."

Felicity felt the cut of Abigail's words. Felicity only wanted to do what was needed.

Abigail glanced in the wagon, where Ben slumbered, finally exhausted. Her hands were folded beneath her cheek, and she looked completely innocent.

It was misleading, Felicity knew.

Taking care of the girl would be a lot of work.

She quickly wrote on the slate, the small piece of chalk dusty and cool against her fingertips. *We'll need more supplies for her.*

Abigail frowned.

Felicity wiped the slate and quickly wrote, *Clothes, food.*

She didn't know what would be left at the other wagons, not when travelers from their company had already gone to collect what they could. She again felt a sting of resentment that she'd been stuck with Ben this morning until August had come and taken the girl.

Abigail shook her head. "The Lord will provide for us."

A fierce indignation caught Felicity by surprise. *Stop saying that,* she wrote quickly, her letters slanting some in her haste.

Abigail bristled.

Felicity erased and wrote again, this time taking longer. Let Abigail wait.

If we want to survive this trip and stay alive in Oregon, we'll have to provide for ourselves.

Abigail's lips pinched together. "You need more faith," she finally said.

Felicity had faith. She believed that God had paid for her sins through the sacrifice of Jesus. But the only evidence she had of him taking care of her on earth was by working with her own hands.

It was just the way things were.

Abigail shook her head again, concentrating a little too hard on folding the towel in her hands. "It's heartless, is what it is," she murmured. "You really want the good men of this company to think you're heartless?"

She nodded to August and Leo, standing at the edge of the circle of wagons, talking.

"You're sweet on August," Abigail said. "What'll he think of you stealing from the dead?"

It wasn't stealing, and Abigail was a fool to think so. Likely, August would agree with Felicity that it was smart to take what supplies they might find. But a niggle of doubt crept in.

Abigail wore a smug little smile when she caught Felicity glancing in the men's direction.

Stung, Felicity wrote, *I don't like August.*

Abigail made a sound between a sniff and a snort.

Felicity couldn't let herself admire August. He was a hero, all right. He'd swept her into his arms, rescued her just yesterday. And then he'd promptly found Ben, the pregnant Rachel, and her brother.

If anything, August collected unfortunate souls.

For a few days, after his heroic rescue of her from the twister's wreckage, she'd thought that perhaps she meant something special to him. Now she was beginning to realize that he was a kind man who cared about people.

Him checking on her, helping her locate a new wagon, bringing the slate. Those things didn't mean anything special was growing between them. It's just who August was.

Whatever disappointment she might've felt was pushed back as Abigail shook her head. "I don't believe you."

Felicity turned the slate toward her, pointing furiously at what she'd written.

But Abigail was smirking, sort of.

Felicity's face heated with embarrassment and indignation. She and Abigail had gotten along all right up until now. But this disagreement was like that quicksand that had sucked at Felicity's feet and legs.

She whirled away, wishing for an escape.

She came face-to-face with August, whose gaze flicked down.

She realized too late that she was still holding the slate in front of her.

Flames licked at her cheeks as she whisked up the slate and used her closed fist to wipe the words away.

Too late.

He'd seen them.

One corner of his mouth twitched. Like he was hiding a smile.

He wasn't angry? Relief unfolded. She quickly wrote on the slate. *Not talking about you.*

"You weren't talking about me?"

Abigail called out from behind her, though she'd gone around the wagon. "Yes, we were."

Felicity wanted to sink into the ground in mortification. Was Abigail going to humiliate her, then?

"She wants to go over to the wagons and find some supplies for Ben. And I told her that you'd think it was a bad idea."

"It's a good idea," August said. "I'll go with you."

When Felicity turned her head, Abigail's lips were pinched.

Maybe August had validated Felicity's need to go, but Abigail was clearly upset by the idea.

"I wanna go," Ben's tremulous voice called out from behind the canvas.

August brushed past Felicity to glance inside the open back of the wagon. "Don't you want to rest?"

"No!"

Felicity barely registered their conversation.

Abigail had flounced off, leaving the three of them

alone. At least she hadn't told August how worried Felicity was about surviving the journey. Those thoughts were private. Felicity had been foolish to share with Abigail. They were friends, of a sort, and she thought Abigail was trustworthy, but Felicity could only count on herself. It had been that way for as long as she could remember.

August turned from the wagon with Ben in his arms. Did the man have an unending reserve of stamina? She'd never once seen him tired, though he must be after having been out late last night and early this morning.

"I'm gonna find my pa," Ben said resolutely.

But a shadow moved in August's eyes. Felicity knew the chance of finding the man alive now must be slim.

She wrote on the slate and held it up for him to read. *Horses?*

He wrinkled his nose. "We don't need a horse. It's only a short walk."

But then he pretended that Ben was much heavier. He made his voice ragged. "On second thought, maybe we do need a horse. Or a cart and pony. How much breakfast did you eat?"

Ben giggled.

"I'll have to see if I can find some branches that we might make into a pair of crutches. What do you think, Felicity?"

Good idea. She thought it a delight to be able to answer him. She was thankful for his thoughtfulness, even if it didn't mean anything special.

"See that?" August said. "You'll be swinging around on your own in no time."

Maddie had seemed worried by the severity of the

break. She'd cautioned to keep the girl as still as possible. But in a week or two, the crutches could help.

The giggles from Ben had dissipated by the time they reached the first wagon. There was a suspicious rust-colored stain on the grass nearby. Felicity came shoulder-to-shoulder with August as they glanced inside the ripped canvas at the back of the wagon.

It had been ransacked—pages ripped out of a book strewn across the wagon bed, marks where a heavy barrel of something had been dragged.

You shouldn't raid their wagons.

Felicity felt a twinge of unease.

It didn't matter. There was nothing left to be salvaged.

They found the next two wagons in the same condition.

Disappointment swamped Felicity. Was there nothing of value left? She was too late, it seemed. She wrote on the slate. *Should we go back?*

August read it and considered. "I noticed last night that much of the supplies were missing from the wagons already."

Was that why—she didn't know how to finish the question and wrote a question mark. Somehow, he understood her meaning. Was that why they'd been attacked?

"I don't know," he said in a quiet voice. "It's a terrible tragedy no matter the reason."

He glanced down at Ben, in his arms, who was scanning the horizon. Searching for her missing father.

"We should go a little farther, if you're able. See if we can't find her wagon and maybe some clothes."

Ben went tense when they neared the wagon where they'd found her.

"Was this the last place you saw your pa?"

Ben nodded. "He was shootin' at the men."

Felicity's heart went out to the little girl. What a terrible thing to have witnessed. She peeked into the wagon. Disappointment swelled as she took in the empty, ransacked wagon bed.

A shadow fell over her as August stepped beside her. Ben had turned her face into his shoulder as if she couldn't bear to look.

Nothing here. She didn't have to write the words. He knew.

"It was a good idea," he murmured quietly to Felicity.

Her gaze snagged on a dark line bisecting the floor. That was a big crack. She'd overheard Rachel talking about a false bottom in her wagon. Was it possible...?

She climbed into the wagon with some effort and wedged her fingers into the crack. August caught on quickly. He shifted Ben into one strong arm, using the other to help Felicity.

The board came loose and Felicity lifted it out of the way.

Underneath were several crates of ammunition.

August whistled. "Now that's a find."

It wasn't food. Or clothes. Or something she could sell. But ammunition could help if they needed to hunt along the journey.

Or protect themselves.

Chapter Eight

"I don't want this. It's disgusting."

Rachel didn't move from her position kneeling at Daniel's side. Partly because it had taken her too long to get down here, and partly because it would be awkward and take even longer to get up.

It was late in the evening. In a few minutes, she'd have to attend the funeral. She already felt raw and shaky.

She gentled her voice. "You need to eat. You have to keep your strength up."

She tried again, extending the spoon with a hearty stew toward her brother.

He turned his head away to stare at the inside of the canvas tent.

She bit her lip to keep words from spilling. It wouldn't do anyone any good if she lost her temper. But it was a near thing.

Daniel's face was pale, but his cheeks were flushed with fever. The healer woman, Maddie, had been concerned about the way his wound had been inflamed, the puckered skin around the edges of the bullet hole red and hot to the touch. If Daniel's wound became infected, he could die. And she couldn't bear the thought of losing her brother, the last of her family.

She'd already lost Evan.

"Won't you just try?" she asked softly.

Daniel only grunted.

The stew wasn't the best she'd ever eaten, but it was palatable. She'd forced down a bowl for the baby's sake.

She wasn't the only one who'd lost it all. Daniel's wife, Glinda, and their young son, Simon, had been slain in the attack. He was grieving, maybe even lost in his grief.

They'd never been close. He was six years older than her and could be mercurial and controlling. It had been a relief to marry Evan, though there had still been times of unhappiness.

Evan had taken them on this journey. Now she was terrified of being alone. Of having this baby in the wilderness when she should've been back in Pittsburgh with the rest of civilization.

She needed Daniel. And he needed her.

Her left leg started going numb. Daniel still refused to look at her.

Fine.

She'd come back in a little bit and try again.

"I'm going to see about getting us some horses or a wagon," she told her brother. "So we can go home." She'd been asking around within the caravan, starting with August. One of the women had snapped at her when she had delved into begging.

Daniel's head thrashed on the pillow, his eyes squinting as he looked at her. "We don't have a home to go back to. We've got nothin'."

Her heart went out to him, even if the bite in his words stung.

"We have each other," she said.

He threw his arm over his face and turned his head away again.

It was a struggle to move her ungainly body and get one foot underneath her. Especially when that foot was half-asleep. She got caught in the tent flap and bobbled the bowl. The spoon dropped to the ground with a thump.

Her stomach hung heavily and brought her off balance. She stumbled.

And a hand reached out to catch her elbow.

She had a ready smile for whatever kind soul had helped her, but when she glanced up, the smile slipped from her face.

Owen Mason. The very man who'd thrown her to the ground so mercilessly when he'd *come to her rescue.*

He released his hold quickly, as if she was a piece of coal that could brand him.

It was on the tip of her tongue to say she hadn't meant his brother harm, but before she could speak, he sniped, "Not much of a thank you."

Her already precarious hold on her temper wavered and snapped. "If you've come to apologize for what happened last night, I don't accept."

She couldn't help glancing down at where the spoon lay on the ground. With her belly so big, she wouldn't be able to reach it without going to her hands and knees. And she refused to humiliate herself in front of him.

He bent and retrieved the spoon, holding it out to her. His eyes were narrowed almost to slits, and a frisson of unease slithered down her spine.

When she tried to take the utensil, he held on for a prolonged moment. Probably so she'd know he was in control of this conversation. "I won't apologize," he said. "You were holding a gun on my brother. You should be the one apologizing."

She knew now that August had wanted to help her, but in the heat of the moment, in the dark, his motive hadn't mattered.

She tipped her chin up stubbornly. "I was protecting myself. Why should I apologize for that?"

"I was protecting my brother."

Drat the stubborn man. She pressed one hand to her belly, where the baby had given a powerful kick. Saw Owen's eyes dart to her stomach and then away. Maybe a shadow had shifted in the depths of his eyes.

Or maybe the morning sun was in hers.

"Excuse me." He motioned toward the tent where Daniel rested.

She stood her ground. "My brother needs his rest."

"And I need to talk to him."

"Whatever you have to say to him, you can say to me."

Her mother would've been appalled at her speaking to a man—or anyone—this way. She'd been taught from a young age to be genteel, polite, stay in the background. But Mama would have never expected to find her out here in the wilderness, among rough men like this.

Owen took off his hat and pushed his other hand through his hair. His face was a thundercloud, but she still couldn't find it in her to be polite.

Perhaps witnessing the death of her husband and being frightened and alone for four days had killed something inside of her. That polite part.

"We're moving out soon," Owen said. Were his teeth gritted? "After the funeral."

The funeral. She didn't want to think about walking over to where the men had been working all morning. About seeing Evan's body lowered into a community grave.

So she forced her thoughts to her current predicament.

"My brother and I think it's best we return to Independence."

His dark eyes considered her. No, he was waiting for her to continue. He was going to make her say it.

Her lips pinched together. "Is there someone else I should speak to?"

"I'm one of the captains for this company."

"Then do you know if there's anyone who would be willing to part with a pair of oxen?"

From what she understood from the snatches of conversation she'd heard since they'd been taken in, there were no supplies found among the wagons from her company. Everything had been raided. Stolen.

She didn't need much. Perhaps a rifle and a few items of game. A pair of horses.

But Hollis's wagon train had been through trials of their own. That tornado had either cost folks supplies or reminded them how precarious things were out here. No one was willing to part with their horses.

And she'd never shot a rifle in her life.

"Every family in this company needs their oxen to reach the Willamette Valley."

"What about a pair of horses?"

His mouth twisted in a disdainful way. "You're going to sit a horse in your condition?"

She didn't even know if she could, but she masked her irritation at his presumption and bared her lips over her teeth in an approximation of a smile. "If I have to."

That twist in his lips remained. "You got any money? Anything of value to trade for a horse?"

He knew she didn't. She hadn't been back to the wagon—hadn't been able to bear facing the site of Evan's murder.

"The way I see it, the two of you'll have to ride along to the next fort. You can get more help there."

"And how far is that?"

He shrugged. "Another two weeks. Approximately."

No! She didn't want to travel so far in the wrong direction. The way she figured, it would be a month, at most, before this babe arrived.

And she had nothing. No husband, no place to live, no money.

Her only chance was returning to Pittsburgh. She had friends there.

"That won't work for us," she said primly.

"It's gonna have to. In the morning, you need to get that brother of yours up and break down that tent. It'll be your home for the next bit."

In that moment, she hated him. Her eyes flashed

when she raised her chin stubbornly. "I'll find a way home. I swear it."

* * *

Felicity bit back a groan as she lugged an armful of sopping wet dress from the washtub to the drying line she and Abigail had strung between their wagon and Evangeline's. When Hollis had called for a halt today, she and Abigail had decided to do some washing.

But it had been a busy day and she was just now finishing, after the sun had gone down. Fires crackled all around camp. Conversations had been quiet since the funeral. Abigail had gone off to help another family. Ben was sleeping in the tent.

Felicity just wanted to join her. Every muscle ached. But this job had to be completed.

The fire in her ribs protested each movement. Only a few more items to be hung. Then she'd have to drag that water bucket outside of camp and dump it.

She glared at the offending bucket.

Tiny voices from nearby drew her attention. Little Sara and a young boy not much older were sitting near the wheel of a wagon, playing pat-a-cake. Evangeline was standing close but had her nose in a book and only glanced up every few moments.

"I'm fairly sure you aren't supposed to be exerting yourself like this." Alice. The soft chiding voice had Felicity hiding a wince as she put a wooden clothes pin on the dress she was hanging. She had her slate in her apron pocket, but it was quicker to simply hold up two fingers. Only two dresses left.

Alice held out a hand. "Give me a couple of pins."

When Felicity relented, Alice took one of the dresses out of the washtub. She gave it a good wringing, moving so quickly and efficiently that Felicity felt a spark of jealousy. She would eventually regain mobility, she told herself.

"I've fallen behind on the mending," Alice said easily as she notched the clothespins over the dress on the line. "I don't suppose you'd have time to help me with it?"

Felicity considered this as she took the last dress out of the tub and wrung it out, much more slowly than Alice had.

"I was thinking..." Alice went on. "Ben will need more than just the one dress."

Felicity nodded. She hadn't thought about that, but Alice was right.

"Weren't you a seamstress?"

Felicity nodded again.

"I've got a dress that is still in good shape. Ben can use it, if you could use your skills to turn it into something her size. We can work together to help her, can't we?" Alice included Felicity in a conspiring smile.

Felicity felt part of the loneliness from days ago lift. Alice was offering her friendship in addition to helping Ben.

What Alice and her family had done for Felicity couldn't be repaid. In those first terrible days after the tornado, Alice had cared for Felicity almost around-the-clock. Evangeline had given her one of her own dresses when Felicity had none of her own to wear. August and Owen had been the ones to find them a new wagon.

Felicity had felt like a burden. But Alice's offer of

friendship warmed her. She finished hanging the last dress and grabbed the slate out of her apron pocket.

Thank you.

Alice gave her a warm smile. "Of course. Let me go get the dress."

She took the tub of water with her before Felicity could protest.

Relief at not having to lift or drag the heavy bucket with her injuries coasted over her as childish giggles floated on the air. Felicity glanced up to find the two children now playing tag, running around the wagon. Evangeline stood on a crate with her head and shoulders in the back of the wagon. She wasn't watching them, though Felicity could hear the cadence of her voice as she called out to them.

A fire remained lit, not far from Evangeline's wagon. When Sara darted around the conveyance, the air she disturbed blew across the flame. The little boy followed her.

Felicity wanted to call out, but she knew it wouldn't matter without a voice. She walked toward the fire as the two children disappeared out of sight, behind the wagon. A happy shriek told her they weren't finished with their game yet.

"I'm going to get you!" A tiny voice cried out.

Felicity hurried the final few steps, but she was too late. Sara darted out from the shadows, looking over her shoulder. Her trajectory carried her straight toward the fire. Felicity's foot slipped in the soft prairie grasses. She reached out, ignoring the twinge in her ribs.

Her fingers brushed Sara's shoulder. Her slight push sent the girl spinning away from the burning logs.

But at that moment, a projectile rammed into Felicity from behind, sending her off balance. With the fire to her left, she couldn't catch herself. She fell, her left arm far too close to the flames.

The little boy had hit her. He'd fallen too, now tangled up in her skirts. She scrabbled to get away from the fire just as a little hiss declared the sleeve of her dress had caught fire.

"C'mere." August. Felicity had never been more grateful to hear that calm voice. "Evangeline!" he called out.

He ripped the boy off of Felicity's legs, grabbed her right arm and pulled her away from the fire. Flames licked her skin, and she cried out silently.

"I'm right here." That same voice she'd heard once before as she had been fighting for her life. Instinctively, she turned toward him.

August clamped his hands over her sleeve, uncaring about the risk to himself.

The flames had been smaller than they'd felt and were out in a matter of seconds. She lay face to face with August, who'd put his back to the fire. She was stunned, panting for breath.

Evangeline had climbed out of the wagon and gathered the two children close. "What happened?"

August sat up quickly and nudged Felicity further from the fire. "Grab some water, would you?"

Alice was there, suddenly. She grabbed the drinking water bucket and dipper.

August pushed up Felicity's sleeve as he answered Evangeline. "I only saw the end of it. The kids were running around. Felicity saved Sara from going headlong into the fire."

He poured cool water over the scalding skin on the underside of her forearm.

"I'm gonna borrow an egg from Nanny Smith," Alice said, darting off.

Felicity glanced over August's shoulder to Evangeline, who was examining Sara.

"Is she all right?" he asked.

"Yes. And she's going to get a lecture about running near the fire." Evangeline moved off with the two children, leaving August and Felicity alone.

"She needs more than a lecture," he murmured under his breath. "You could've been burned far worse."

He poured another dipper of water over her arm. She could feel the strength in his fingers, gentle on her wrist. He put down the dipper and used them to gently push up her soggy sleeve, now with a hole burned in it. There would be no patching a hole of this size.

He turned her arm to get a better look at the wound. She looked too. An angry burn already marred the skin, the size of two of her fingers side by side. Another scar, only two inches above, winked silver in the dancing firelight. It was usually hidden beneath the sleeve of her dress, but now his finger brushed over the old scar tissue.

"Stove?"

How had he known? She nodded.

She'd been making dinner, when she was about twelve, and a large pot of boiled potatoes had slipped. She had tried to catch it. The underside of her forearm had touched the stove. Celia had barely looked at it before issuing a command for Felicity to get the dinner on the table.

Felicity thought August would let go of her. The burn wasn't too bad. It wasn't blistering. But he helped her up, brushed off her skirts, and ushered her to sit on one of the crates near the wagon. Then he went to meet Alice, who'd rushed back into their little corner of camp. He said something to her that Felicity couldn't make out with his back turned. Alice glanced once more at Felicity and then left, heading in the direction where Evangeline had disappeared.

August strode back, something small and white held in one hand. The egg.

As he walked, the lines of his shoulders beneath his shirt rippled with muscle and made a twist in her stomach that wasn't entirely comfortable. She lowered her eyes and chided herself. He was only being kind.

"My ma taught me this remedy when I was small," he said as he knelt in front of her. "I showed it to Alice a coupla weeks ago when she burned her hand."

He carefully punctured the top of the egg and cleared away the shell until there was an opening big enough for his finger. He dipped his index finger in and then motioned for her to show him the burn again.

"The egg white creates a protective film over the burn," he murmured as his finger brushed the clear liquid over her arm so gently that she barely felt it.

Except that she felt it everywhere.

"If it blisters, you'll want to bandage it." His voice was as gentle as his touch, and she blinked rapidly, attempting to distract herself. August was a friend. That was enough.

The silence stretched between them, somehow fraught with a fine tension that seemed almost tangible. Finally, he cleared his throat and stood up.

"You've got a good heart," he said.

His words warmed her even after he'd given her one final smile and gone away, even after she was tucked in her bedroll inside the dark tent.

She never wanted to forget that feeling.

Chapter Nine

Early in the morning, after he'd finished scouting the route ahead, August approached Hollis's wagon. Even before the incident where Hollis had received his concussion, the wagon master had separated himself from the rest of the caravan by angling his wagon and erecting a tent where it blocked him from view. Unless you came looking for him, his area was private.

Today August was looking for him.

August rounded the wagon and found Hollis sitting on the ground with legs outstretched, a small circle looking glass in hand and a lather for shaving in his lap. He had a straight razor in his other hand.

Chest cinched tight, August tried to draw a breath that wouldn't come. Owen was going to be angry when he found out about this.

"You got a minute?"

Hollis flicked his eyes at August before his focus returned to the mirror. "What?"

94

The curt answer was the usual for Hollis. He wasn't one for long, involved conversations.

"I think we should move the caravan away from the river." He went through all of the same explanations he'd given Owen, praying that the wagon master would see sense.

Hollis's eyes never wavered from his focus on that mirror. When August finished laying out his argument, there was only the *scritch, scritch* of the razor at Hollis's throat. He was still staring into the mirror when he finally said, "You have a falling out with your brother?"

"No."

It seemed like minutes passed before Hollis wiped the razor on a towel laid over his thigh and finally looked at August. "Then how come you aren't talking to him about this?"

Tension twined around August's neck and shoulders. "I have. He doesn't see the danger."

August had hoped to find an ally in Hollis, at least about the danger the buffalo represented.

"The group voted on Owen as one of the captains," Hollis said.

Something twisted inside August. His brother had tried to push him to be one of the captains, but he'd refused. He couldn't be responsible for all the souls on this wagon train.

"Your brother is a reasonable man. Why don't you try talking to him again?"

Frustrated, August took his leave. Hollis wouldn't listen. He'd already tried to talk to Owen. August didn't like that his warnings were disregarded. He knew he had a history of not making the best decisions, but not this time.

Why wouldn't they listen?

He rounded Hollis's wagon so caught up in his thoughts that he nearly ran down Rachel.

He caught her shoulders in his hands, set her gently back. She let out a breath and pressed one hand to the side of her belly.

"Sorry," he said. "I wasn't looking where I was going."

"That's all right." She smiled sweetly at him. "You're a difficult man to catch sitting still."

She'd been looking for him? "Is everything all right? You getting enough to eat?"

"Yes. I do need to ask you something, though."

He nodded for her to go on.

She inhaled deeply, as if it was difficult for her to get the words out. "Daniel is still too weak to walk."

"Of course. He'll ride in our wagon. Owen's and mine."

Was it his imagination, or did her gaze fly over his shoulder?

When he turned to look, he caught sight of Owen across camp, speaking to Leo. He knew Rachel and Owen had had words yesterday. Everyone in camp knew it.

August had watched her during the funeral, dry-eyed and pale. Most folks would have sought out Owen for help, as captain. But she'd come to August.

"We're happy to help you," he said.

The twist in her lips said she didn't quite believe him. He would just have to prove her wrong. "What else do you need?"

"I've spoken to several families in the company. Unless you've got a spare wagon and oxen team, I doubt you can help any more than you already have."

He shrugged his helplessness.

She straightened her spine and glanced over his shoulder.

"You tryin' to talk to Hollis?"

She nodded.

He tipped his hat and moved out of her way, leaving him to muddle through more thoughts on why their caravan should outpace those buffalo. He needed something for his hands to do.

He went to check on the oxen, where they'd been picketed for the night. He'd just ran his hands down the spine of one animal and was bending over to lift its foot and check the hoof when he became aware of someone approaching.

Owen.

"They all right?"

"Dunno," August replied. "I've just started checking this one."

It was on the tip of his tongue to remind his brother of his worries, argue for changing their route again. But after Owen's last dismissal, he swallowed the urge and kept his head down.

"Saw you talking to Rachel."

Now his brother was keeping tabs on him?

"Did she say anything to you?"

"About what?" August grunted the words, releasing the hoof he held and making his way to the ox's back end to do the same.

"I don't know. She's a harpy."

His brows crunched together, but he didn't lift his head. There was a little swelling around the ox's hoof. With his thumb, he brushed aside some dirt to look closer.

"What's that supposed to mean?" he asked when Owen didn't go on.

"She's got an argument for everything. Stubborn as a mule. She's infuriating, is what she is."

"I told her Daniel could ride in our wagon since he's too weak to walk."

Owen scowled. "He needs to get up. It's not good for him to lie around so much."

"I'll encourage it," August said easily.

Owen didn't argue further, but his scowl remained.

Let him stew a little. It was rare for him to be so wound up over anybody. Owen was a born leader. It was rare for anyone to stand up to his confident demeanor and sure nature. But Rachel had sure gotten under his skin.

Maybe it made August the ornery younger brother, but he was going to enjoy this. At least for a few moments.

"What she needs is a strong-handed husband to keep her in line," Owen muttered. And then he went silent.

Suspiciously so.

"You picked out anybody to go courting with?" Owen asked the question casually, but August's hackles went up.

"Not yet." After all, he'd been busy with scouting and rescuing and what not.

He stood up to go get a paste to put on the ox's hoof.

Owen fell into step beside him as he headed toward their wagon.

"That baby'll be coming before we hit the rockies, I reckon'. What's she going to do then? She needs a husband."

August slanted a glance at him. Owen sure had thought a lot about that baby for someone who claimed to be irritated by its mother.

"You want to have an infuriating woman be a part of the family?" he only used the word because Owen had and he wanted to bother his brother.

Owen frowned fiercely. "Maybe she'd settle if she was married to you."

"You really think a woman will change?" Of course, he'd seen her forceful, argumentative side when she'd been hiding behind that gun.

Owen made a noise of disgust. He pointed a finger at August. "You better keep your mind on courting. We'll hit the Willamette Valley sooner than you think."

August glanced away, let his eyes rove the horizon.

He'd been having second thoughts ever since he'd made the agreement with his brother. In most things, Owen knew better, and he trusted his brother's judgment.

But this was personal.

And maybe a little painful.

When August thought of waking up next to someone for the rest of his life, it was Felicity's pretty face that appeared in his mind's eye. He quickly blinked that image away.

Felicity was a friend. She trusted him. They were working together to take care of Ben.

Best not change things. Not now.

* * *

"I need a drink."

Felicity ignored the plaintive call from inside the wagon and focused on the needle and thread in her hands. The sun was making its descent toward the horizon. Her light would run out soon enough.

Maybe it was too early to put Ben to bed, but Felicity needed a break from the child's constant demands. At breakfast, Ben had been whiny and refused the fried egg and skillet biscuit she'd been given. She'd jarred her leg at a mid-morning jaunt to have some privacy in the woods and cried for a half hour, only settling back in the wagon when Abigail had read her a story from a book Evangeline had loaned them.

All afternoon, Ben had asked Felicity whether her father had been found yet.

Felicity hadn't had the heart to tell her that her father was probably dead. It was the one relief in not having her voice back.

Before they'd pulled out at mid-day yesterday, after the funeral, August had taken her aside and told her no one had seen any sign of Ben's father, dead or alive. He'd wanted Felicity to be ready for Ben's grief because somehow, though she couldn't speak to her, Ben had decided Felicity was the one person in camp that she wanted.

"Felicity!" the call threatened to turn into a wail.

Felicity pushed the needle through fabric with more force than was necessary. She caught her opposite thumb with the tip of the needle and winced, quickly sticking the digit in her mouth to soothe the sting.

She kept sewing. Surely Ben would tire enough to fall asleep soon.

Felicity knew the little girl wasn't that bad. She was smart as a whip and curious. She'd been cajoled into helping Abigail stir the pot during supper preparations and had been so proud of herself when Leo had walked by and heaped praise on her.

Even so, there was a part of Felicity that rebelled against the necessity of being tasked with watching over the little girl. She had finally gotten free of all the entanglements she'd left behind in Pennsylvania. She was no longer a servant in her own household, taking care of children that weren't hers. She still held herself carefully apart from Ben.

But maybe she wasn't so thick-skinned after all, because her heart pricked when she heard the quiet sobs, muffled in the back of the wagon.

She put two more quick stitches into the fabric before tying off a knot in the thread then using her teeth to break it. She stowed the needle carefully in the small tin—now dented from its ordeal in the storm—and stood up.

Ben's cries decreased when Felicity stood on the back wagon wheel to peer inside the shadowed wagon bed. She held out the item in her hand—a small rag doll. Alice had helped her paint the face and donated some yarn for hair.

Ben slowly reached out to take the doll. Her eyes were big and wet with tears that seemed to have stopped for the moment. She touched the doll's hair, ran a finger down the stuffed arm. Then she clutched the doll to her little chest, squeezing tightly.

"Thank you," she whispered.

Felicity rubbed Ben's arm until she seemed to be dozing, then carefully extricated herself from the wagon and stepped down to the ground.

She held on to the wagon side for a moment, her other hand going to her face, fingers pressing against her eyes. She sent a little prayer heavenward that Ben would sleep through the night. She hadn't yet, the pain in her leg often waking her. Or maybe nightmares.

Did the girl's subconscious somehow know that her father was gone?

When Felicity looked up, she caught August's gaze from across camp. He was walking with a barrel on one shoulder. He nodded to her, and she gave a little wave.

Her stomach tightened. She hadn't seen him since yesterday morning. Hadn't talked to him. He'd been moving around camp. Working. Probably looking for someone else to rescue. She tried to tell her heart to stop wanting him so much.

It hadn't helped.

Now she wandered past the wagon to the outside of the circle made by their caravan. She'd wanted to range farther from the wagon train all day but couldn't because of Ben. Now was her chance. Even if the little girl didn't sleep all night, Felicity could have a bit of freedom. Couldn't she?

She turned her head and saw the new addition to their wagon train. Rachel.

The pregnant woman stood between two wagons, not quite out in the open. She was looking into the distance, in the same direction Felicity had been thinking of walking.

Felicity patted the large pocket of her apron, where she'd stashed the slate August had given her. She took it everywhere with her now. She approached Rachel, who had her arms wrapped around her middle—as much as they would reach.

When Rachel saw her approaching, she brushed a hand over her cheek.

Felicity took out her slate and wrote, *Want to walk?*

Rachel's eyes scanned the words and then raised to Felicity's face. "I've been standing here for far too long trying to gather the courage to fetch some firewood on my own. I'd be thankful for the company."

They set off at a moderate pace. Felicity was grateful. Most everyone walked so fast that Felicity's ribs ached with each step. It didn't hurt nearly as badly walking at Rachel's pace.

Rachel glanced sideways at her. "Is it. . .I've been trying to think how to ask in a way that isn't rude. Have you always been mute?"

Felicity wrote as she walked, which was more difficult than it should've been. She nearly twisted her ankle when she stepped in a low place. Then she turned the slate toward Rachel. *No. Tornado. Wagon fell on me.*

She pointed to her ribs and throat as Rachel's eyes widened.

"We saw the storm—it was terrible. I didn't know there was a twister." She looked frightened for a moment, then she turned her face away and composed herself. "What a miracle that God spared your life."

Her words stopped Felicity's whirling thoughts.

She'd spent almost three weeks blaming God for putting her in this predicament, injured and with no money and supplies, dependent on the charity of others. Had she even stopped to be thankful that she was alive?

Shame seeped over her.

They reached the shade of a wooded area and Rachel exhaled noisily. She fanned her face with one hand. "I overheat so easily now," she said by way of explanation.

They turned to follow the edge of the woods, keeping the wagon train in sight. Suddenly Felicity realized someone had followed them from camp. For a moment, Felicity's heart leaped at the thought that it was August.

Instead, she saw a man she didn't recognize. He was limping, clearly favoring one leg.

Rachel must've followed the direction of her stare. She frowned. "That's my brother."

She went to meet him while Felicity continued on, slower.

"You find me a horse yet?" His voice rang out clearly over the quiet prairie. His words dripped with condescension or maybe anger.

Rachel glanced in Felicity's direction.

Felicity moved off a little more. She could barely hear Rachel's response, spoken in a much lower tone. "There are no extra horses to be bought. And we have no funds to buy one anyway."

"I cain't walk," he said angrily.

He'd walked to follow them out here, hadn't he?

"The wagon master said perhaps we'd have some luck at the next fort."

He growled, the sound sending a feeling of anxiousness down Felicity's spine.

Her eye caught on something up ahead, in the lengthening shadows cast by the stunted trees. It was square. A shape that didn't belong out here in the wild. She was happy to outpace the argument that got louder behind her.

She felt compassion for the brother and sister, of course. Their situation was similar to hers. Dependent on the charity of others. But they hadn't lost only their physical belongings. Rachel had lost her husband, and Felicity had heard whispers that Daniel had lost his wife and small child.

They were both grieving. It was forgivable that tempers were short in such a tragedy.

She hurried to what she could now see was a chest. An expensive one, with carved patterns in its edges. *Please don't be empty*, she thought as she reached for the lid.

A lizard slithered away into the grass, and she jumped. She closed her eyes, praying there weren't more of the creatures inside. She lifted the lid.

Inside were piles of dresses. Some fancy. Some everyday wear. They were fresh, smelling as if they'd been washed not long ago. Someone had left them behind, but it had to have been someone traveling this season. They weren't faded one bit.

She might've hoped for food supplies or a cache of gold coins, but this was something. The fabric could provide clothing for Ben. Rachel. Even Abigail and Felicity. She'd found something of value. And there was no one to claim this but her.

She gathered the pile of fabric into her arms and stood. Holding the bundle made her ribs ache, and it was hard not to trip on the long skirt of one dress that hung low as she walked back to camp.

Rachel and Daniel were still arguing. She left them there, not wanting to embarrass her new friend. She needed to find out if there was anything in the clothing that might make a peace offering for Abigail.

Chapter Ten

Two days later, they'd left the site of the massacre far behind. They'd had sunny weather and traveled over fifty miles. Hollis called for an early stop and a late start the next morning.

Felicity sat on an overturned crate near her wagon, Ben at her side. It had fallen dark, but the travelers didn't seem to care. They'd carefully arranged the fires in the middle of the circle of wagons. Leo played his mouth organ, Collin his fiddle. But Owen wasn't playing his usual guitar tonight.

Music wafted over the gathered people. Suppers had been shared with neighbors and everyone seemed in good spirits.

Including Felicity.

Ben was perched on a crate with her head laid on her arms on Felicity's lap. Her injured leg was resting on another, smaller crate in front of her.

Maddie had been happy with the girl's healing and had put her in a plaster cast. As promised, August had found two branches in the perfect shape for crutches. He'd stripped off the bark with a knife and sanded them down. Then he'd fixed fabric secured with leather straps to the top of each crutch.

Just yesterday, Ben had taken to them like a duckling to a stream. Felicity had had a time keeping up with the girl as she'd scampered through the wagons as they'd rolled along and around camp when they stopped. Ben was constantly searching for her father. Still, almost a week later.

Felicity had tried to tell her in the gentlest way possible that her pa was in Heaven now, that he wasn't coming back, but Ben stubbornly refused to believe her. She made numerous denials until Felicity had finally given up, at least for the time being.

It was definitely more pleasant in camp with a little girl who was content and mobile. Though Felicity knew that couldn't last forever.

Ben twitched as a piece of the fabric Felicity was stitching tickled her ear. Felicity moved her arms, twisting a bit more to the right. It wasn't the most comfortable way to sit, but she wanted to finish this sewing project tonight.

Abigail was visiting with some folks several wagons over. Felicity wouldn't be surprised if she joined in the dancing before long.

Everyone loved Abigail. And tended to forget that Felicity was a part of this wagon train at all.

She pushed away old remembrances and became aware of noise from somewhere behind her—a shuffling of feet. She was stationed in front of the wagon wheel, away from the conveyance itself. Before she could turn around, someone bumped into her from behind, dislodging Ben.

She looked up, ready to reprimand someone for their clumsiness—silly of her, since her voice still wasn't cooperating—when she registered Daniel, Rachel's brother. His withering glare told her he blamed her for being in his way.

Why was he walking around her wagon, anyway?

"You should say sorry!" Ben called when he was several steps away.

He glanced over his shoulder, still glaring, and grunted wordlessly.

Felicity smoothed Ben's hair as the girl settled again, this time with her chin on her folded hands. Felicity didn't have the heart to explain that Daniel reeked of gin. Would he have any remembrance of bumping into them?

Felicity tried to refocus on the sewing in her hand, but her eyes tracked Daniel of their own accord. He stumbled once more before he found Rachel talking with Stella and Collin near their wagon. The music drowned out his words, but it was clear from his posture that he wasn't speaking kindly to his sister. And that Rachel was trying to placate him. Felicity had imagined that same look on her own face many times as she'd tried to cajole her younger brother into sweeping the floor or bringing firewood inside or walking faster so they would make it to the schoolroom on time.

Daniel didn't appear to want to be placated.

Collin said something, and Daniel bristled. Rachel reached out to touch his arm, but he shook off her hold. And then August was there, tall and imposing, but utterly calm. He smiled at Rachel, gave Daniel a thoughtful look, and then whisked Rachel into the group of folks who were dancing in the very center of the circled wagons.

Felicity lowered her eyes to the square of fabric now clenched in her fingers. It took some effort to relax them so they would work again. She pushed the needle through the cloth several times before she glanced back up.

Her gaze went unerringly to August and Rachel. Rachel was smiling at him. Wisps of her blonde hair had come loose from the bun at the back of her head and her cheeks were sun-kissed.

She was beautiful.

And watching her with August made something ache deep inside Felicity.

She lowered her eyes again as she registered approaching footsteps, this time from the direction of the frolicking travelers.

It was Owen. He nodded hello to Felicity and squatted in front of Ben. "Did you get some of the roasted walnuts?"

Ben nodded enthusiastically, the motion interrupting Felicity's needle.

Owen's attention shifted to her. "No time for merriment?"

Maybe she would've had a quick response, if she'd been able to speak. But she only shrugged and motioned to the basket of white fabric at her side.

"What're you making? Napkins?"

Ben giggled. "She's making diapers for Mrs. Rachel's baby."

Something shifted in Owen's eyes and the smile he'd

been wearing twisted. "Isn't that nice?"

But something in the way he said it wasn't.

She didn't understand his strange tension. Thankfully, his attention returned to Ben. "I came over here to see why you aren't dancing, young lady."

Ben sat up straight, bumping Felicity's elbow so that she nearly stabbed her forefinger.

"No one asked me!" the girl said.

"I'm asking." Owen whisked the girl into his arms, mindful of her cast, and they headed to join the fun.

And left Felicity alone with her work.

She told herself it was fine. She was used to it. Work was useful, and she liked being useful. She hadn't come across any other treasures or supplies, but every day she kept her eyes peeled as she walked beside the caravan.

She would keep the promise she'd made to herself. Find a new home in Oregon. There would be plenty of work to do there, too, but she'd be the master of her own destiny. It would all be worth it.

A shadow fell, blocking her view of her stitches. She glanced up to find August where his brother had been only moments ago. Rachel was nowhere in sight.

"Come and dance with me," he said.

She shook her head, motioning to the basket, then what she held in her hand.

"That'll keep, won't it? You've been sitting here all evening. You're missing all the fun."

He'd noticed?

Something about his gentle reprimand made heat flush her cheeks. She thought he'd been too busy rescuing damsels in distress to see her sitting over here.

She put her project in the basket and reached for the slate on the ground right beside it.

I don't know how to dance.

She flipped the slate so he could see the words. His eyes moved as he read, and then his mouth quirked into a smile as he glanced back to her face. "I don't either. It's just moving around."

He stepped closer and extended his hand. She felt a moment of panic. She didn't want to make a fool of herself.

"If you aren't having fun in a few minutes, I'll walk you back over here."

She gave in, taking his hand. He helped her stand up. Then he readjusted his hold so her hand slipped around his elbow as they approached the dancing crowd. How did anyone move amongst all those bodies without getting kicked or stepped on?

But August only grinned at her as he lowered his arm and faced her. He took her left hand in his right one and gently placed his other hand on her waist. He raised his eyebrows, and when she didn't protest, he said, "Just follow me." Then he whisked her into the crowd.

She was too aware of his hand at her waist, the warmth of his skin seeping through the fabric of her dress, the roughness of his palm against hers, to notice the other people around them. The music swelled, and she glimpsed his stubbled jaw as he made sure they didn't stumble into anyone else. He was a good leader. Her feet didn't stumble once.

"All right?" he asked after a few minutes. His eyes were dancing in rhythm with her heart. She nodded, unable to smile, her heart knocking against her ribs as it was. And then he guided them out of the noisy, laughing crowd. They were still face to face, and she was breathless from the dance. Or from the man?

And then he let her go.

"Would you take a walk with me?" he asked.

* * *

August didn't know what he was doing.

He couldn't say what had brought his feet toward Felicity when she had been sitting on that crate. Maybe it was the glimpses of her expression in the flickering firelight. A determined tilt of her lips. Determined to what...? Not be lonely while sitting by herself?

He didn't want her to be lonely.

Or maybe it was the breath of relief he felt after days of safety. They hadn't seen the giant herd of buffalo since yesterday. It was too soon to say so, but he hoped they had outpaced the animals. Things had been calm, and he felt the same relief and joy as everyone else celebrating tonight.

But it was something else entirely that made a pleasant dip in his stomach when Felicity threaded her arm through his and followed him out of the firelight and beyond the wagons into the quiet night.

The music faded behind them as the sky unfolded a brilliance of stars like a blanket of diamonds. A shadow moved, black against the darkness, and he squinted into the night. It was Terry Shaw, one of the men on watch, a hired cowboy Leo had brought on at the last fort. Hollis had agreed, after what they'd witnessed, that this was no time to let their guard down.

August waved to the man and set his pace at a slow meander around the circle of wagons. He wouldn't stray too far.

Felicity was quiet—and not for the first time, he wished he could remember her voice.

Had he spoken to her before the accident? Surely, he must've. In camp? At a river crossing?

"A mending fairy borrowed a couple of my shirts off the drying line," he said after silence had fallen for too long.

She tipped her head to the side. In the moonlight, he could just make out her features. The slope of her nose, the too-innocent raise of her brows.

"She returned them to our wagon, the little tears all stitched neatly. Folded."

She was struggling to keep the innocent facade. He could see the way her nostrils flared, ever so slightly.

"You wouldn't know anything about that, would—?"

He didn't quite get the question out before her left leg twisted underneath her, and she stumbled. He turned and caught her at the waist, her hand now resting on his shoulder. Her held breath rushed out on an extended exhale. He felt the warmth of it on the skin just above his shirt collar.

"All right?" Was that really his voice, that deep rumble?

She began to nod, but then twisted slightly at the waist—he felt it because his hands were still on her hips, and she gasped softly. Even if she'd brought the slate with her—which he knew she'd left behind because he'd watched her—it was too dark to read anything. He had to guess what had happened.

"Tweak your ribs?"

She nodded slightly. She was holding her breath again. He could feel her tension beneath his hands. He didn't know what possessed him to do it, but he slid his right hand up so that his fingertips just brushed the bottom of her ribcage.

"Here?" He barely breathed the word.

She nodded slightly. He knew the right thing to do would be to step back, to put an appropriate, friendly amount of distance between them. But that wasn't what he wanted to do.

Her hand flexed on his shoulder, the tiny movement sending shock waves through him. He let his hand slip from her ribs to rest on her back, nudging her a scant inch closer. Now her breath fanned his chin. The starlight reflected in her eyes and the moon limned her skin with silver.

He wanted to kiss her. More than anything he'd ever wanted in his whole sorry life.

He bent his head, his eyes were sliding closed, when he caught her slight wince.

He stopped.

"Is this a mistake?" The words seemed barely a breath.

His head reared back. Were his ears playing tricks on him? But he could have sworn he'd heard the words, not read her lips.

"What did you—say that again," he demanded.

She swallowed hard. He recognized the anxiousness in her expression. He cupped her jaw with his hand.

"Are you sure about this?" Her whisper was as clear

as a bell this time. Happiness slammed into him as they realized in the same moment that she'd spoken!

He tried to push away the sting of disappointment at the content of her first words as he pulled back. "I heard that!"

She pressed both hands against her cheeks, and his happiness matched her own as she voiced her thoughts again.

"I can speak." Still little more than a raspy whisper. And she winced as the words came out.

"Don't push it," he cautioned. "Your vocal cords are healing, right?"

She shrugged, helpless and still full of joy.

And he swallowed back that disappointment all over again.

Are you sure about this?

He'd been sure, in the moment. But maybe her hesitance was a good thing. He reached up and rubbed his neck.

"Did you really want to kiss me?" She glanced down shyly.

"Yes. I—I think so."

He wasn't looking at her but seemed to feel her disappointment at his answer. Was this another wrong choice?

"I don't want to hurt you," he said.

Her shoulders straightened. "My hurts aren't your responsibility." She sighed and looked up at the stars. "You carry too many responsibilities already. Why do you make yourself responsible for everyone else?"

Tension squeezed his neck. "Habit."

She looked at him until he felt compelled to answer.

"I guess the most recent example is my friend Hank."

He wasn't going to talk about this, was he?

"Tell me about him," she whispered.

He wanted to refuse, but this walk had been his idea, hadn't it?

"We pooled our funds and went in together on a gold mine. We worked together most days." He sighed. "Owen thought it was a bad idea from the beginning. Mining is dangerous enough on its own, but there are also some bad characters drawn to the business."

This next part was difficult to say. "I'd gone home for a few days to see Owen and my pa and when I got back, there'd been a cave-in. Hank was nowhere to be found— until we started digging. He'd been buried alive."

Her hand on his arm startled him. He'd been back in that tunnel, light slanting the wrong way, his pick tearing away soil and gravel to reveal Hank's sleeve.

He realized he was trembling all over. He didn't like to think about that day. Or the days after, when he'd had to bring Hank's parents the news that their son was dead. Owen had stood beside him, stoic, but August knew that underneath his brother's mask, Owen was thinking how he'd told August not to do it from the beginning.

Felicity stared up at him in the moonlight. Her eyes were luminous with unshed tears, and he regretted saying anything at all. Hank was his burden to bear.

And so was Ma.

Felicity threaded her arms around his neck, pushing up on tiptoe, and there she was in his arms. She pressed her lips to his with zero hesitation.

Her lips were soft and tasted like the sweetest wild strawberry. His nose pressed into the delicate skin of her cheek and he breathed her in. A scent that would forever be burned into his brain as Felicity.

She stepped back and his arms fell away. Was she going to tell him that kiss had been a mistake? That moment of connection between them felt like the only thing tethering him to the earth right now.

She turned her head. "Did you hear that?"

The only thing he'd heard was the pounding of his pulse in his eardrums. He strove to calm his breathing, strained to listen. The sound came again. A tiny cry. An animal's cry.

"We should leave it alone. Never know what you'll find out here."

But she'd already moved several steps away.

The cry came again, at the same moment he caught her arm in his hand.

Then he saw the tiny form twitching and cowering, heard the hiss.

"It's a kitten," he said dumbly.

She was already kneeling in the grass, reaching out one hand.

"It's skin and bones," she whispered.

He squatted beside her. "Where'd it come from?"

She didn't look at him, totally focused on the kitten. In the darkness, he couldn't make out the color. Maybe cream, or yellow. "People abandon things all along the trail."

Things. Not animals. Most travelers had the kindness to put an animal out of its misery if they couldn't care for it, not leave an innocent kitten in the wilderness to get eaten by something bigger.

Felicity made some kind of smooching noise, but it

was when August silently extended his hand that the cat laid its ears flat and slowly walked forward to sniff his hand.

"Of course," he thought he heard Felicity whisper as he scooped it up.

Finding this hungry, orphaned kitten meant their alone time was over.

Chapter Eleven

Aug"s heel was chafing against the inside of his boot.

He'd been damp for forty-eight hours. The wagons had pulled all day yesterday in a drizzling rain. They'd barely gone five miles, thanks to the wet weather and the fact that their road had turned into a soggy mess. The rain hadn't let up today, either. The wagon wheels and horse's hooves had kicked up mud that covered his slicker and dotted his face and hands.

He was tired, hungry, and sore.

But it was that hot spot inside his boot that was getting to him.

August was riding out wide of the wagons, near the middle of the train. Water dripped slowly from the brim of his hat. Surely Hollis was going to call a halt soon.

Suddenly, one of the wagons nearby lurched. He was already guiding his horse in that direction when it happened again.

The wagon's wheels had caught in the mud and refused to move.

He waved to the next wagon in line, encouraging them to move past the wagon now floundering in the mud. Collin, also on horseback, had witnessed the problem and used hand motions to communicate that he was riding up to inform Hollis.

Collin wasn't related to August directly, but August genuinely liked the man. He was a good sort. His twin, on the other hand...

There wasn't time to think on it. August jumped down from his horse and asked the driver, a man he didn't know well, whether he had any loose boards they could use to try to get the wheels unstuck.

No go.

More men gathered. Soon enough, August found himself ankle-deep in the soupy mud, his shoulder pushing against the back of the wagon. When another man joined, August looked up through the mist to see Owen shoulder in just behind him.

Someone between the driver and men pushing counted, "One, two, three!"

A slap of reins on oxen, then the wagon jerked.

August's feet threatened to slip in the mud.

The wheels moved about two inches.

"Rachel has been pestering everyone," Owen muttered, low enough that only August would hear.

August wanted to throw his head back and close his ears, but he forced himself to stay focused. On another day, when he wasn't so weary, he might've enjoyed seeing his brother so irritated by the fiery mother-to-be.

August himself was looking forward to settling in for the night. With the wagon train moving at a snail's pace and Hollis asking him to do extra scouting for the route ahead today, he'd barely seen Felicity. He wanted to sit by the fire with her, find out how she'd fared huddled in the wagon all day with Ben. Not listen to Owen whine while they were huddled up next to this wagon.

Owen must've taken his silence for assent that he wanted to keep listening.

"First, she was asking if anyone would sell their horse, now she wants someone to take her hunting."

August pushed with all his might when the count came again. The wagon moved a few inches but then rolled back again when they stopped.

Muscles aching, he shook his head. "What is she thinking?" he threw the words over his shoulder.

"Who knows?"

She hadn't told him specifically, but it couldn't be that long before her baby would arrive. Her belly was big and round, and August didn't see how a person of her size could get much bigger. And she wanted to hike out into the wilderness and shoot a gun? She was so slight she might get knocked over by the recoil.

From his few interactions with her, he knew she was an intelligent woman. What was her intent with the hunting? She had to have some plan.

"Hollis told me several folks have complained about her, so when I saw her walking around and asking the menfolk to take her hunting, I asked her to stop."

August put his hands on the wagon bed in anticipation of the next count. Someone had found some burlap bags to lay in front of the wheels. They would give it one more try.

"I told her you'd take her."

August jerked, his head turning fully to his brother for the first time.

Owen looked as miserable as August felt, his eyelashes damp and sticking together, his face caked in mud splatters.

"I'm not taking her hunting," August said. What if the baby came when they were away from the safety of the wagons? It was a bad idea all around.

"I promised her you would," Owen argued.

"*I* didn't promise," August said.

Facing his brother this time, he saw the frown lines around Owen's eyes, the way he gritted his teeth.

Owen didn't like to be argued with.

The count happened, but he'd hardly been paying attention. He gave a shove a half-second behind the other men.

The wagon lurched forward and the motion took August and Owen and the others forward a few steps and then they fell behind as the wagon rolled off.

Owen parked his hands on his hips as he stared at August. "You're missing the point here. Spending some time with her. Alone." He glanced around, finally seeming to realize they were surrounded by other men. Men August didn't want knowing his business. "*Alone*," he repeated with emphasis. "That will give you a chance to get to know each other. See if you suit."

Owen had brought up the idea of August marrying Rachel once before. August had barely considered the idea before he'd tossed it aside. Felicity was the woman he wanted to get to know better.

Felicity was the woman he'd kissed.

And he rather wanted to do it again.

The other men mounted up and rode off, leaving August and Owen standing, squared off.

"I can manage my own affairs," August said now.

"When?" Owen pushed. "I haven't seen you make any attempt to get to know a young lady from the caravan."

August opened his mouth to tell his brother about his growing feelings for Felicity. Then he snapped it shut. Did his brother really need to know every single decision in his life? Owen hadn't been paying attention the other night when August and Felicity had gone walking.

"You're dawdling," Owen said, pointing his finger at August.

"I'm not." It wasn't a crime to want time to think about things. Getting married was a big decision.

Owen started to respond when August beat him to it. "I still don't understand why you're pushing me at Rachel when you don't even like her. You really want to share our camp with her for another three months? Or more?"

Owen pulled a face before his lips firmed in determination. "You'd be the perfect person to settle her. Easygoing and steady."

August didn't feel easygoing. He felt like shouting his frustration at his brother. Or maybe at the sky.

"I promised her you'd take her tomorrow, while you're scouting, before we roll out." Owen walked off, as if that was the end of the conversation.

And why shouldn't he? August had let his older brother dictate his decisions for a long time.

Frustration roiling inside him, August stalked over to his horse. He felt like a wild mountain cougar was gripping its claws into his back and shoulders. He put his hand on the saddle horn but didn't haul himself into the saddle.

If he let Owen push him, he'd end up married to Rachel before the week was up. Owen had a burr under his saddle about that woman. August got along with her just fine. But he didn't feel one iota of what he felt for Felicity.

Yet he'd trusted Owen to make decisions for him when he couldn't trust himself. In the wake of Hank's death, August could've disappeared into a bottle. Or into the wilderness. Just taken off.

It was Owen who'd pushed him to help Pa with the homestead. Owen who'd insisted they go East to find their long-lost siblings. And August had started coming out of his grief on that trail East.

Now he felt the uncertainty of navigating this life-changing decision. He'd made that bet with Owen in the heat of the moment. Owen knew how much the family homestead meant to August.

If he went along for the sake of peace, would Felicity get her feelings hurt? They'd shared a kiss, but there were no promises between them. And if August made the wrong decision here, it could hurt Felicity. Maybe even hurt Rachel. Make things difficult with his brother.

He could do things Owen's way, but did he really want his brother to make every important decision for him in the future?

Was Owen going to decide the name of August's

firstborn son? Would he know when it was time to add on to the house? What crop they should plant?

It left a bitter taste in his mouth.

But wasn't it for the best?

* * *

Felicity woke with a start. Heart pounding, she strove to get her bearings.

She was in the tent. She could hear the patter of soft raindrops against the canvas roof.

She wished it would stop raining. There was no storm, no flashes of lightning or rolling thunder, but the relentless rain made everything feel wet. Clothes. Socks inside of shoes. Even the air felt cloying when she breathed it in.

It was still pitch dark. It must be the middle of the night. There were no noises of camp waking up, and even the birdcalls and night insects had gone quiet.

What had woken her? Had Ben made a noise?

She reached out her hand to touch the girl's bedroll, between Felicity and Abigail.

The space was empty. The bedroll was rumpled and cool to the touch.

"Ben," she whispered.

Only Abigail's even breaths in the silence answered her.

When she called out again, a little louder, Abigail stirred.

"Ben is gone," Felicity whispered, thankful that her voice had come back enough for that, that she wasn't trying to mime her worry to Abigail in the darkness.

"Mmm. Maybe she went out to use the toilet."

In the dark? Alone?

Felicity had been woken by the girl on numerous occasions for something as minor as a pain in her leg, a glass of water, a frightening dream.

Why hadn't she woken Felicity tonight?

Unease stirred.

"Abby?"

Her tentmate made an incomprehensible noise and rolled away.

Fair enough. Felicity had been tasked with keeping Ben while Abigail had spent much of the evening nursing a young mother who'd fallen ill with a fever. Things hadn't been the same with Abigail since the disagreement they'd had. Felicity had offered to take in one of the dresses she'd found for Abigail, but her friend had claimed she didn't need another.

Now Felicity felt around in the darkness for her shoes and quickly laced them up by touch. If Ben had gone out on her own, she could be lost.

Outside the tent, she was immediately pelted with the same steady, drizzling rain they'd endured the past two days. Whatever semblance of dryness she'd had in the tent was immediately gone. She wished she'd grabbed her coat, but there was nothing for it now.

Her first step slipped a little on the soggy ground. She steadied her feet, knowing a tumble might wrench her side. They'd visited a copse of woods not far away to take care of personal business before bed, so she headed that way, arms crossed in front of her to try and conserve warmth.

She called Ben's name every few steps, her whisper-voice not carrying far in the rain that seemed to mute everything. She made it to the woods but could see no sign of the tiny girl on crutches. She stood for a moment, now sopping wet, fuming. She turned a slow circle, calling softly, "Ben!"

Nothing.

A branch snapped nearby, and her heart jumped inside her chest. "Ben?" This time her whisper emerged tremulous.

Was someone out there? Someone bigger than Ben?

She wished she'd thought to wake August or one of the other men. Instead, she'd walked out into danger all alone.

They still had someone on watch, didn't they?

Maybe she was overreacting. The nighttime silence had returned. She heard only her erratic breaths. She needed to think clearly. If Ben had come out here to use the toilet, it was possible she'd gotten lost.

Felicity remembered August's search pattern from when they'd scouted the other wagon train. She would search for a short time, and if Ben wasn't found, she'd get help. She was turning to make her way along the tree line when a dark figure loomed over her.

She started to shriek, but her vocal cords protested with a cutting pain. All that emerged was a squeak.

"It's me." A gentle touch at her elbow and the familiar cadence of his voice overcame the heart-stopping fear.

August.

"I was on watch and heard you call out. What's wrong?"

It took a moment for her to catch her breath. He cupped her elbow in his hand and shielded her body from the rain with his. Just having him close was a comfort.

"I woke up and Ben was gone from the tent. I don't know where she is. She usually wakes me—"

He shushed her with a squeeze of his hand on her arm as something crashed through the woods nearby.

An animal?

August started off that direction and, wise or not, she trailed him.

"It's her," he said over his shoulder.

"Felicity!" the wobbling voice urged her faster. She outpaced August for the final steps.

There was Ben, on one crutch, her white nightgown plastered to her body.

Felicity went to her knees, uncaring that her nightgown would be muddy. She clasped the girl to her. "What happened? Did you get lost?" She leaned back to be able to hear Ben's answer.

"I thought I saw Pa out here in the woods. I came to find him."

Felicity struggled for a moment to understand. Maybe it was her sleep-addled state. "You mean, you dreamed about your pa?"

"No! I saw him." Ben's voice wobbled and a soft sob escaped. "Tonight, when we was getting ready for bed, I saw him."

That wasn't possible. Felicity felt a surge of anger at being woken for this, for the fear and worry she'd experienced, for getting all wet.

All for nothing.

"No, you didn't."

"Yes, I did!" Ben's voice rose and wavered.

"Your Pa is dead. He's never coming back." It was the fear and worry talking, the anger and sleeplessness making her words sharp.

Ben stared at her. Her lip trembled, barely visible in the darkness. "You don't care. I heard you complaining about me 'afore. You don't want to take care of me, an' I want my pa back!" Ben's voice broke.

Felicity felt frozen.

"Hey." August knelt beside them.

She'd forgotten he was even here, for a moment.

He wrangled them so he was sitting on the cold, wet ground, Felicity snuggled to his side, and Ben across their laps. Ben was shaking and crying.

"It's late, and we were scared something happened to you." August's voice was calm and even Felicity felt herself breathing easier at his words. "We can figure out what happened in the morning. What's important is you're safe."

Ben pressed her face into the side of his chest, her body wedged into the place where Felicity was snuggled into his side.

Somehow, he'd tucked the side of his coat behind her. It didn't enclose her, but with the added protection and his arm around her shoulders, he was sharing his warmth.

But it didn't quite touch Felicity.

You don't care. I heard you complaining.

Ben's words were like an arrow to her heart, cutting and deep.

How many times had she thought those very same thoughts about her stepmother? Father, too? They'd been caught up in their new family, father in his work, too many mouths to feed. Celia had been notoriously self-centered. Felicity had often felt that neither one cared about her. Neither one loved her.

And it was a terrible thing to believe.

She'd been so reluctant to take on the care of Ben, so focused on finding supplies and goods to ensure her own future beyond the wagon train, that she'd never considered that she had the power to make Ben feel the very same way she'd felt as a child.

Shame trickled over her like the rain still pouring down. Ben didn't deserve that. She was alone in the world, and for whatever reason, she'd gravitated toward Felicity. Did Felicity want to continue as they had been? Barely tolerating each other? Did she really want to be like Celia? Callous and uncaring?

She didn't like that thought. *No.* No, she did not want to end up like that.

August's arm tightened around her shoulders. He must've tipped his head because the scruff at his chin caught in the wet hair at her temple.

"It'll be all right."

Ben's sobs had tapered off, and now her ragged breathing was the only sound.

Felicity reached her arm around the girl, her fingers brushing August's opposite arm where he'd also wrapped Ben in his warmth. Felicity hugged Ben as best she could.

"I care about you," She whispered into Ben's wet hair, pressing her face there.

Ben had no one—she needed a mother. Felicity wasn't old enough to be her mother, and she didn't know what the future would hold. She didn't have enough funds or food to make it to Oregon. But she was going to do everything she could to be the big sister Ben needed. She made the vow to herself and in a silent prayer to God.

She and Ben would stick together.

And if there was a silent addendum to the prayer, a tiny begging voice from her heart that asked for August to be a part of their lives, she would never tell a soul.

Chapter Twelve

*O**wen said we cain't eat supper with the Teller family no more.* The words her brother had growled at her on their short break for a cold lunch had Rachel riled up into a righteous temper. Evening was falling and Rachel wanted nothing more than to rest. She didn't want supper, didn't want to wash up. Just sleep. But she hurried her stride, at a near run as she outpaced the wagon at the front of their caravan.

The wagon master had told them this morning that today would be a push. He wanted to make up some of the miles they'd lost over the last days slogging through rain and mud.

Fine. The sooner they reached the fort, the better.

But then had come Daniel's grumble. *Cain't eat supper with the Teller family.*

Who was Owen Mason to tell them what they could and couldn't do?

For certain, he was one of the captains and thus, in

charge of their company. Much to her distaste. But to refuse them the common decency to eat with one of the families that had befriended them?

It was infuriating.

She'd been stewing ever since Daniel had told her about it, and as the evening wore on, she'd decided to confront the captain.

Unfortunately, he'd been riding out in front of the wagon train for most of the day. Now he was in her sights, his horse slowing. Surely, they were almost finished with today's travel.

She'd started the morning riding out early on a borrowed horse with a quiet August beside her. They'd intended to go hunting, hopefully find a deer or turkey. Instead, they'd found the plain littered with buffalo as far as the eye could see. August had insisted on riding back to the company as fast as possible. Whatever he'd said to Hollis, the wagon master had blown the bugle before anyone was ready to pull up stakes for the day.

Why couldn't Owen be more like his brother? Kind, patient, compassionate. As far as she'd witnessed, Owen had none of those qualities.

"I need to talk to you!" she called out.

Owen gave one glance over his shoulder, then looked forward again.

She was within shouting distance. "I know you heard me."

Between her hurried steps and her shouts after him, she was out of breath. Not to mention the baby seemed to steal the very oxygen out of her lungs. She put one hand beneath her belly as she pushed herself to a near-run for a few more steps. "Owen Mason!"

She saw him glance heavenward as he wheeled his horse and approached, slowing to a walk. As she opened her mouth to demand an explanation, his brows crinkled and he held out a hand to stop her.

The nerve of the man!

Her temper boiled higher—

But then a strange noise registered. Like the rumble of far-off thunder. But the sky was clear and cloudless, the sun throwing colors as it set ahead of them.

Owen was staring behind and to the north. A look of horror dawned on his expression.

She whirled to see—

And beheld hundreds of buffalo stampeding over the horizon and down the plain—straight toward the wagon train.

It was almost mesmerizing, the way the shaggy brown bodies flowed, moving together like water on a flood plain. But then the ground beneath her feet began to shake.

Owen shouted something at the wagon closest behind her. He took his hat off his head and waved it. She looked around frantically, as if the earth might sprout a house made of stone, something strong enough to protect her, protect the baby inside her.

Of course, no such miracle appeared.

"Take my hand!" Owen's bossy voice barely preceded his horse sidling up to her. The animal had wide, fearful eyes, showing the whites. It was dancing beneath him, and she was afraid of the hooves.

"Now!" he roared.

She reached up and he grabbed her forearm, quickly pulling her into the saddle in front of him. She sat side-

135

ways across the horse's back and he made no move to seat her more comfortably.

The roar of hoofbeats gained on them as he spurred the horse into a gallop—in the wrong direction. He was headed back toward the wagon train, toward the stampeding animals.

"Get into the wagons!" he shouted at those nearest to him.

He hadn't secured her on the saddle, and she nearly slipped off. Then one strong arm came around her enormous middle.

"We've got to run!" she cried, but her voice was drowned out by the pounding of hooves against the ground.

And then it was too late.

He wheeled the horse, almost unseating them both as the animal dug its hooves into the earth at a full run.

The horse sprang into a gallop in front of the buffalo —and was almost instantly overtaken.

She screamed as one of the animals pressed against the horse's side.

Owen grunted. Had his leg been smashed by the beast? Then the buffalo moved away slightly and crashed into the animal on its other side.

Rachel was both sobbing and screaming, unable to catch her breath. All it would take was one misstep by the horse for it to lose its balance, for the riders to tumble to the ground. They would die beneath the buffalos' hooves—

"Easy." Owen's voice came in her ear, low and gentle, a tone she'd never heard from him before.

Dark spots were dancing on the edge of her vision,

and she couldn't draw breath. Maybe this was the way she would die—

"Rach." That tender purr couldn't be Owen's voice. Only her mother had used that nickname. She should berate him for it, but she still couldn't fill her lungs.

"It's gonna be okay."

"H-how—" She barely got the word out, garbled so he surely didn't understand it.

"My gelding can run like this all day. Can you take a breath for me?"

She hated his highhandedness and would tell him so —but his calm reassurance helped somehow, and she was able to find the space to draw one breath. Only belatedly did she realize that she was clutching his shoulder with a white-knuckled grip. Surely, she was bruising him. She took another breath and tried to let go.

"Why don't ya blast me the way you were rarin' to do a minute ago?" His voice was tinged with laughter.

She hated him in that moment. How could he make fun of her when they could die if he lost concentration?

She took a shuddering breath. "How dare you tell Daniel we can't eat supper with the Tellers?"

Her words would have had more punch if her voice had stopped shaking. She was still clinging to him, and she felt a fine tension string through his shoulders.

"I didn't tell him that. I told him he has to stop drinking after supper."

Heat flushed her neck and into her face as she realized Daniel had misled her. It didn't stop her from saying, "You don't have the right to tell him what to do. He's grieving his wife and child—"

"I do have the right. He needs to start pulling his

weight. You two might not have a wagon, but you can't just rely on the kindness of others—"

"He's still injured," she spat back. Now she had to deny the impulse to strangle the man. He made her so mad!

She recognized the change in pace as he slowed the horse. The sound of the buffalo had dulled. The herd had stopped running. She lifted her head to peer over Owen's shoulder. A sea of brown, shaggy bodies surrounded them. One nearby shook its head menacingly.

"Owen!"

"I see it." His voice held the same disdain she heard every time he spoke to her.

She must have imagined the gentleness earlier. It had been loud. She'd misheard. It hadn't been real.

He pushed the horse to a trot until they were a dozen yards away from the nearest buffalo.

There were no wagons in sight. No other riders.

Only a herd of animals that seemed intent on killing them if they got too close.

"What do we do now?" she hated the tremble in her voice.

"We've got to get back to the company." He sounded so reasonable and sure. As if there was a company to get back to.

It only took a few minutes of riding at a walk to witness the churned ground where hundreds—thousands?—of hooves had pounded over it, chopping up the turf.

"Do you think anyone was hurt?" She closed her eyes against the thought, but her imagination showed an image of the herd careening right over a wagon and whoever would have been inside it.

"I don't know." His tone was grim. And it was falling dark.

* * *

Felicity walked several feet away from the wagon, Ben swinging along beside her on her crutches. Somewhere along the trail today, one of the spokes on the front left wagon wheel had broken. The wagon listed slightly to the right, and Felicity had decided it was better to drive the oxen from the ground, rather than the wagon seat.

They had started out the day near the front of the company, but now they lagged well behind the last wagon. She knew one of the men would help her mend the wheel once they made camp. She prayed and prayed that the wagon would make it that far.

Limping beside her, Ben wore the kitten in a small sling pouch that Felicity had sewn for her. After days of drinking milk that one of the families had donated from the cow, the kitten had grown stronger. Ben adored it, took it with her everywhere, though the kitten had a special affinity for August.

"D'you think there'll be cows in Oregon?" Ben asked.

"Yes." Felicity's voice had gained the slightest bit of volume today, but she still barely got over a whisper. The pain in her ribs was finally abating, now only a dull ache that she could mostly ignore.

"What about rabbits? Will there be rabbits in Oregon?"

"I think so." She didn't rightly know, but surely there were.

"Will August live nearby, when we get to Oregon?"

Ben's innocent question made Felicity's heart lurch. "I don't know."

Ben had been a chatterbox all day. It was as if she'd totally forgotten about the events of last night. Meanwhile, Felicity couldn't seem to stop thinking about Ben's insistence that she'd seen her father.

It had to have been a dream, didn't it? Even with the new travelers in their company, Felicity had learned the faces of everyone on the wagon train. She hadn't seen anyone out of the ordinary that evening. But neither had she been paying as much attention as Ben, the girl still hopeful of finding her father alive.

And Felicity also couldn't stop thinking about August. About the way he'd surrounded both her and Ben with his calm presence. About the way he'd brushed a kiss against her hair as he'd left her at the flap of her tent. Or had she imagined the gentle touch?

This morning, she'd been making breakfast with Abigail when she'd seen August meet Rachel outside of camp, near the horses. Rachel had been all smiles, even tilting her head in a way that had made Felicity's stomach twist uncomfortably. Then they'd ridden off into the sunrise.

And Felicity had been left to wonder what they were doing. Why they'd gone off alone.

Were they courting?

Rachel would need a husband, what with a baby on the way and no wagon of her own. And Felicity already knew August wanted to marry.

Was there some agreement between them?

She'd resolved to talk to him, but when he and Rachel had ridden back into camp, Hollis had given the signal to pull out in such haste there'd been no time.

She'd kept her eye out for August today as Abigail had driven the wagon. He must've been ranging far from the train of wagons because she hadn't had one glimpse of him. And she desperately wanted to see him. To bask in his calm presence and pretend that everything was all right.

There were shouts from up ahead. Felicity looked up to see Leo standing on the back of his wagon waving wildly at her. She raised a hand slowly, uncertain as to why he was shouting.

Then a loud rumbling started up. And the ground began to shake.

"Felicity!" Ben shrieked.

She whirled and saw the marauding buffalo. They were everywhere, heading straight toward them.

"Get in the wagon!" Her raspy whisper wasn't audible over the growing thunder of buffalo hooves, so she waved frantically at Ben.

From the corner of her eye, she registered a rider on horseback racing toward them.

Whoever it was would never reach them in time.

Ben got close enough for Felicity to grab her and throw her into the wagon seat. Ben's crutches flew wildly away, and the motion wrenched Felicity's side. She cried out, the sound nearly silent. Then she scrambled for the wheel, the wagon still in motion.

The buffalo were almost on top of her now. She braced for the coming impact. Before the wild animals reached her, the horse she'd seen coming pulled up at the back wheel of the wagon.

August.

His eyes were wild. "Get on!" he shouted.

She scrambled for a hold, finally pulling herself up into the wagon seat.

"Get in the back," she told Ben. The girl must've registered the fear in her voice, but she struggled to open the closed canvas cover.

August rode until he was at Felicity's side, dangerously close to the wagon wheel.

"Push them faster," he called over the noise around them.

"I can't! The wheel is busted."

A buffalo bawled. She jumped, even as she slapped the reins to urge the oxen faster. One of them mooed plaintively. The wagon rocked. A stampeding buffalo must've run into it. From inside, Ben screamed.

August pushed closer to the wagon. The animals must be pressing in on him too. His horse was balking, its eyes showing the whites.

The oxen tried to jump in their traces, but she slapped them again and they kept moving.

August looked behind as the animals kept flowing around them. "A little farther. Keep it steady."

But she felt the wheel listing even more. If the wheel broke completely, they would be stranded out here.

If the rampaging buffalo didn't trample them first.

"A little more!" he called out.

Fewer and fewer buffalo pressed in on them.

And then it was just the stragglers.

The herd had outpaced them, still running, leaving a choking cloud of dust behind.

Afraid the wagon wheel would bust, she reined in the oxen.

August halted his horse and looked at her. "You all right?"

She shook her head in the affirmative. And then in the negative.

It took a moment to pry her nerveless fingers from the reins. That was long enough for August to dismount, get his feet on the wheel spokes, and reach for her.

She threw her arms around him, welcomed the feel of his strong arms surrounding her as she sobbed all the pent-up fear into his neck. She felt his hand run over her hair, cup the back of her head.

"You all right, Ben?" he asked.

Felicity didn't have the wherewithal to look up, but he must've reached out for the little girl, because her cast banged against the wood of the seat and then Ben was pressed against Felicity's back.

"We're all right." August's voice sounded a little rough. He pressed his jaw to Felicity's head.

Ben let go first, with the resilience of youth. "What were those?"

"Buffalo," August murmured. "Remember when we saw them a couple days ago?"

Felicity let go, using her sleeve to mop her face. She winced at the pull in her side.

August stroked her cheek. "I saw you toss her up into the wagon. Hurt yourself?"

"Only a little."

Ben was still focused on the animals, leaning over the edge of the bench to watch them run away. "I only saw 'em from a long ways away. I thought they was small!"

"They're plenty big," August said. He and Felicity shared a glance that seemed to say everything—that the animals were frightening, and they were glad to be alive.

"How come you were so far behind?" he asked.

"Something's wrong with one of the wheels," she said. "Abigail walked ahead to get some help. We figured we could fix it after we stopped for the day."

He looked ahead of them in concern. The rest of the wagons were now out of sight.

Felicity felt a burst of worry for her friend. Had Abigail been able to get to safety?

"Let me look at it. We need to catch up with the company."

Dusk was falling, and Felicity felt a shiver of unease. "Are you worried about the buffalo coming back?"

She saw his fierce frown before he turned his head. "I'm worried about what spooked them. I've been watching them for weeks. Never seen them run in a panic like that."

"What could frighten an animal that big?"

She followed him around the wheel, where a spoke had broken completely, making the wheel appear oval inside its rim. Not good.

"Nothing good," was his only response.

She wrapped her arms around her middle.

She was glad for August's presence. Seeing him ride up, having him come to her rescue just solidified what she'd been thinking about all day.

She was going to ask him if he'd consider marrying her.

They could be a family, August, Ben, and her.

But this wasn't the time, not when he was squatting next to the wheel, examining the break.

Would she ever be brave enough?

Chapter Thirteen

"I don't wanna go to sleep. What if the buffalo come back?"

Felicity smoothed Ben's hair back from her forehead. "Mr. August doesn't think the buffalo will come back."

The orange kitten was awake and feeling playful. From its spot inside the crowded wagon bed next to Ben, it swatted at Felicity's sleeve. August was working to try and repair the wheel. He had suggested Ben be put to bed inside. If he could fix the wagon, she wouldn't be disturbed while they caught up to the rest of the company. No one had come for them. Felicity worried about how the other travelers had fared.

Now she gently disengaged the kitten's sharp claws. She redirected the kitten to an open space in the corner, where a tiny bit of yarn waited. "Besides, the faster you fall asleep, the faster it will be morning. When you wake up, we'll be reunited with the rest of the company."

Felicity sent up a fervent prayer that it would be so.

She could hear the muffled sounds of August's work. Every once in awhile, the conveyance jostled slightly. One little spoke in the wheel had caused a whole heap of trouble.

"Don't worry. Everything will be all right. Soon enough we'll be back with our friends." She placed her hand on a crate to lever herself up off the floor of the wagon bed. The kitten pounced on her hand, tiny claws digging in.

"Ow!" She got to her feet awkwardly in the small space, hunched over because the canvas roof meant she couldn't stand straight. She scooped the kitten into her hands, clutching the squirming ball of fur to her middle. "I'll take this little one with me for a few minutes so you can go to sleep."

She'd like to set the little furball free on the plain to fend for itself.

The wagon jostled an inch or so as she climbed out the back. When she clung to the side for balance, her ribs felt as if a hot knife sliced through them. Her feet hit the prairie grass and she sucked in a breath as she waited for the pain to abate.

The kitten squirmed and Felicity struggled to hold on to it. She would've let it down on the ground if she could've bent over. And then August was there, the warmth of his hands enclosing hers for the briefest moment before the kitten was lifted away.

He stood close, one hand coming to rest at her lower back as she panted through the pain.

"Wrenched it pretty good, huh?" he asked gently.

She could only nod.

"Will the kitten run away?" she whispered.

In the darkness, it had slipped under the wagon and out of sight.

"Nah. It's a smart little thing. It knows you're the one providing milk every morning and night."

The night was quiet around them, a cricket chirping from the tall grasses somewhere nearby. August's hand moved up her back and around her shoulder. He gave a gentle tug so that she was leaning into him, letting him take some of her weight.

Warmth rose up inside her, overtaking the cold fear that had settled like a boulder in her gut since the frightening events of the afternoon.

"I'm afraid the news isn't good," he said.

She leaned her head until it rested against his shoulder. She could see the side of his jaw and the strong column of his neck.

"The wheel is busted?" she guessed.

"The wheel is busted." He didn't sound aggravated. Maybe she was the only one feeling this way.

"I've been thinking it over," he went on. "You got anything of value in the wagon?"

He probably already knew the answer. "Only sentimental value."

He squeezed her shoulder lightly. "I could ride out to try and locate the rest of the company. Bring someone back who can fix it."

Her stomach twisted at the thought of him riding off and leaving her alone with Ben.

"But I can't stop thinking about what might've happened to spook those buffalo," he said. "I've seen a pack of wolves make an attempt on a lone animal. The buffalo charged and scared off six wolves. They aren't scared of much."

What was he saying? "Are you saying something bigger than a wolf frightened them into that stampede?"

"Six wolves," he said gently. "I'm wondering if my memory is playing tricks on me. Just before the stampede came over that rise in the prairie, I thought I heard far-off gunshots. Several of them."

She shuddered. "You think a person caused the stampede?"

Who would do such a thing? She remembered the terrifying moments when they'd been surrounded by the beasts, when the wagon had been knocked into and rocked dangerously.

"Someone could've been killed."

"Another reason I'm not sure I should ride off and leave you. I don't know what happened to the rest of the company. If there were injuries, or worse..."

Then there might not be a camp to get back to.

Maybe it was the concealed emotion of what she'd been through driving that wagon, residual fear at the thought of Abigail or another friend being killed beneath the hooves of those beasts...

Whatever the cause, she couldn't help turning her body into August and burying her face in his broad chest. Her arms went around his back and his went around her shoulders. A few tears seeped out of her closed eyelids.

"I'm being silly," she whispered. She didn't even know if he could hear her with the words muffled in his shirt.

"It's not silly to be afraid." He said the words into her hair. "When I saw your wagon lagging behind and thought I wasn't going to get to you in time..." He trailed off and when he spoke again, his voice was ragged. "I can't stand the thought of anything happening to you."

Her heart leaped. It wasn't a declaration, not exactly, but it was what she needed to hear right then.

They held each other for a quiet moment. Her fingers clutched the fabric of his shirt; she felt the press of his hands against her shoulders. It was as if they needed this time to reassure themselves that they were both alive and safe.

When he spoke again, his voice was a rumble in her ear. "It might be best to put you and Ben on my horse. I can walk. We can all head back to the company together."

He leaned back slightly, his hands cupping her shoulders so that she had a clear view into his face. "You think you can sit in the saddle for as long as it takes us to find them?"

She thought about the mauled ground, the trampled grass. There would be no easy way to look for tracks from the wagons, not after the buffalo had affected the entire area. They didn't know how far the wagon train might've been swept forward, or how far she and Ben had lagged as the wagon wheel had failed.

It could take hours. All night.

She firmed her lips so the tremble in them wouldn't betray her. "I can do it."

It would be incredibly painful. Her ribs would pull with each movement of the horse. Her nose stung with tears just thinking about it.

Somehow, he seemed to see through her. "Hurts that bad, does it?"

She tried not to show anything in her expression, but when she went to shake her head, a single tear broke free and spilled down her cheek. He brushed it away. For one breathless moment, she thought there might be a repeat of the kiss they'd shared once before.

But he turned away. Moved to the back of the wagon and rifled inside for a moment. Then he murmured, "C'mere."

He settled in the grass with his back against the wagon wheel, one he'd put a wooden block in front of earlier so it couldn't roll. He tugged her down gently beside him.

She tried to protest. "I thought—"

He tucked her into his side. "You thought I wouldn't know just how bad your ribs are hurting? I watched you tiptoe around camp for weeks, trying to hide how much pain you were in."

He had?

She didn't know what to do with that realization, couldn't wrap her fuzzy mind around it as he tucked a quilt he must've taken from the back of the wagon around them both.

A shadow darted out from beneath the wagon. The kitten. It attacked his boot where his feet were stretched out in front of him.

"All right?" he asked.

She hummed assent. Being held next to him like this made the pain fade to a dull roar. But his gentle care stirred up old hurts, and she found herself wiping away more tears.

"What's this?" he asked, pushing aside her hand in his

gentle manner then sweeping away her tears with his thumb.

"Nothing."

"Your tears are not nothing. Did I hurt you?"

"No." She knew him now. August would do anything, even put his life at risk, to keep her from being hurt or in danger. "It's just been a long time since someone has taken care of me like this. Or maybe this is the first time."

"Not even your parents?" His question was a whisper in the darkness.

"They provided a roof over my head, food to eat." For a long time, she'd believed that was enough. "But I was usually the one taking care of all the children."

* * *

Felicity's voice was so small in the darkness. And her words carried an old hurt that made August want to gather her close. But he was also conscious of her injuries. He didn't want to exacerbate her busted ribs. So he settled for closing his opposite hand over hers on their laps.

Her head lolled against his shoulder.

It felt deceptively peaceful. The buffalo had pushed Felicity's wagon into a depression in the land, where they were almost obscured from the prairie surrounding it. But those buffalo were still out there. And whatever— or whoever—it was that had scared them. He couldn't let down his guard.

"I raised chickens for awhile," she went on, "when I was a teen. Scrimped and saved all my egg money. I'd had my eye on this beautiful shawl at a shop in town. I'd saved almost enough money, so one afternoon, after I'd walked to town to fetch my younger siblings from school, I checked the jar where I kept my savings and found it gone. My stepmother had used it to buy fabric for new dresses for my younger sisters."

She said the words in a matter-of-fact manner. As if what had happened was expected or that she'd accepted it. But he was angry on her behalf.

"She shouldn't have taken your money."

Her hand left his for a moment as she brushed her cheek. The kitten had stopped wrestling with his boot and now made its way up August's leg, sniffing his pants. When Felicity lowered her hand, she hesitated before slipping it back into his. She seemed to be holding her breath.

Did she think there was a chance he didn't want to hold on to her?

This time, he threaded their fingers together. He felt the intimacy of the gesture in the prickles that went up the back of his neck, into his hair.

Felicity started breathing again.

"I would've given her the money if she'd asked," she said, and it took a moment for him to track back to the conversation.

"Of course, you would've. You've got a generous spirit."

Maybe she'd sensed his indignation on her behalf because he could hear the smile in her voice. "You think so?"

"'Course. Look at you with Ben. You sewed her that doll, spent countless hours up with her in the night. You've helped Rachel and Alice. And me."

He felt the hesitation in her next breath. As if she wanted to say something but didn't. Then he was momentarily distracted by the kitten curling up next to his thigh.

Felicity settled into silence, which gave him a chance to try to marshal his thoughts. He had overheard her talking to Abigail once, knew her parents were still alive. He'd wondered. Of course, he'd wondered what had sent her on this journey west all alone.

Sounded like her parents were a piece of work. Hadn't they appreciated her at all?

Her head tipped and leaned against his shoulder. She'd relaxed. Might even be dozing off.

He should be doing something. Trying to figure out a fix for that wagon wheel—two new spokes would do it—or unsaddling his horse so the animal could have some true rest.

But August felt stingy. Maybe it was selfish to stay in this moment, snuggled with a beautiful woman and that ornery kitten, finally still.

He wanted more nights like this.

A far-off noise trickled over the quiet night. Voices, sounded like. Disembodied, still at a distance. He didn't get up; remained still and breathed evenly, though he let his eyes roam.

Down in this bowl of a depression, the voices could be coming from any direction. The shape of the land meant a bit of an echo. They faded out.

He squeezed Felicity's hand and she roused, her breathing quickening.

"*Shh.* Somebody's out there. I heard voices." He barely breathed the words.

"Men from our company?"

He had an itch in his gut that cautioned him to tread carefully. "I dunno. I'm going to go check it out."

He felt the tremble that passed through her. He brushed a kiss to her cheek and stood up, careful not to rattle anything on the wagon.

The moon wasn't out yet, and that meant maybe the wagon would be hidden enough down in this depression that someone riding by in the night wouldn't see it. He jogged to his horse and pulled the rifle from its scabbard on his saddle. Took it to Felicity, still sitting on the ground. She recoiled when he put it across her lap.

"Just a precaution," he whispered. "I've got my revolver."

He left her, moving swiftly on foot in the direction he thought the voices had come from, which he thought was generally the direction the buffalo had gone. Would Hollis and the company have been swept this direction in the stampede?

He stopped for a moment to listen again and heard nothing.

Had it all been in his imagination?

Unease tightened his gut.

Hollis was smart. He'd suspect that something had frightened the buffalo. If the wagons were intact and there were still able-bodied men to do it, Hollis would've circled up the wagons tight.

The question was, would he have sent out a search party?

August had streaked past two wagons at the rear of the company when he'd spotted Felicity's wagon so far behind. Someone would've told Hollis and Owen that

August had gone after them. Would they trust that he could bring them back safely? If it wasn't Hollis's men out here, then who was it?

He came to a tree line and paused again.

There.

This time it was the whicker of a horse. He crept along the line of trees, spotting the shadows of several horses, men on their backs.

It wasn't a search party. They seemed to be waiting for something.

August couldn't get close enough to determine their identities, not without revealing himself. But if Hollis had sent out a search party, the men would've had makeshift torches, been spread out, shouting for survivors.

These three men were hiding.

He was trying to decide whether he should try to sneak closer or go back the way he came when the sound of branches snapping and soft thuds of hoofbeats met his ears.

More men.

He counted five more, all shadows in the darkness. One passed close enough to where he lay flat on the ground amidst leafy undergrowth that he smelled horse and unwashed flesh.

They must've drawn up closer to his position than the others because he could make out some of their words.

"...didn't work."

"... wagons circled up."

One complaint was loud enough for him to make out clearly. "I almost got trampled by that buffalo—all for nothing."

Their words ran through his mind.

A plan that didn't work?

Buffalo.

Wagons circled up.

Had these men caused the stampede? If so, they'd put the entire company in danger.

"They're shaken up. Prob'ly won't even set out a watch tonight."

He felt a rush of relief. Most of the travelers must be all right if they'd circled up the wagons. But these riders, strangers to the company, were talking about whether there'd be a watch set up...

It suddenly made an awful kind of sense. These had to be the men who had attacked the smaller wagon train that Ben and Rachel and Daniel had traveled on. They'd caused the stampede, possibly to get August's company discombobulated and maybe spread out from each other.

Did they intend to murder and rob his company, too?

Shaken, he tried to listen to their plans, but they spoke quieter and soon moved off.

There wasn't time to think. The evil men were moving opposite the direction he'd come from. Once he got far enough away to be out of sight in the darkness, he sprinted toward Felicity's wagon.

"It's me," he called out as he neared.

Felicity must've set the rifle against the wagon. She was standing and she caught his arm when he stopped next to her, struggling for breath.

"I think it's the same men who attacked the other wagon train."

Felicity gasped softly and then listened as he told her what he'd overheard and his suspicions.

She seemed as frightened as he was.

"They'll be caring for the wounded and trying to fix up any broken wagons," she said.

"And Hollis and Owen and Leo will have no idea that anyone is out here and coming for them." He couldn't stand to think it. If the bandits got close enough to sneak into camp, they could have guns blazing while the travelers slept.

"We have to warn them," she whispered. "You have to warn them. Ride back to save them."

He shook his head. "I can't leave you and Ben out here unprotected. Once the sun comes up, you'll be in plain sight."

He'd seen what those men had done, how they'd killed in cold blood. It wouldn't matter to them that Felicity and Ben were female and vulnerable.

He clutched her to him fiercely. "I can't do it. You matter too much."

She clung to him with the same fervor. She must be terrified. She'd ridden into that scene with him.

"We have to do something," she murmured tearfully, finally pulling back. Her chin jutted up. "Put me and Ben on the horse, like you said before. We'll ride to camp and warn everyone."

Her idea sparked inside him. "If you're on the horse, I can go after the men on foot. Scare them by coming from the flank. Maybe delay them long enough for you to get to camp."

There was no time for a tearful goodbye, not with their family and friends in danger.

She woke Ben. August put them on the horse. Ben insisted on holding the sleeping kitten wrapped in her skirt. Felicity insisted August keep both rifle and revolver. Then she caught the shoulder of his shirt in her fist, leaned down from the saddle, and kissed him fiercely.

He tried not to see the tears streaking down her cheeks as he slapped the horse's rump. As it disappeared over the rise, August set out at a dead run.

Chapter Fourteen

Felicity ducked low over the horse's neck, her body shielding Ben's, as they rode toward the circled wagons, their canvas tops white against the darkness.

Just like August had told her to.

The position put pressure on her ribs. Pain streaked through her like tongues of fire, licking through her flesh over and over again, causing tears to seep from her eyes.

Tears of relief also streaked her cheeks. She hadn't been sure she would be able to find the wagons, though August had guessed the general direction where they might've ended up after the stampede.

Everything was quiet. No gunshots rent the night air. Maybe everything would be all right. But she couldn't stop thinking about August out there in the night, armed and ready to put himself between evil men and his brothers and friends.

Someone shouted as she rode right through the

nearest two wagons and reined to a stop, almost unseating herself.

"It's me!" she tried to call out, but her voice cracked.

The kitten started yowling, and she heard a sound like the hammer of a gun being cocked—

"Hold up!"

Leo! She almost burst into relieved tears at hearing his voice.

He came out of the shadows, flickering flames backlighting him. His brother Coop was at his shoulder.

"Where's August?" Leo demanded.

She straightened in the saddle and cried out, dropping the reins to press her hand against her side, where fire bloomed and pulsed.

"She's hurt," Coop said. "Give me the little girl."

Ben howled as Coop brushed past his brother and nudged Felicity's leg to pull Ben out of the saddle.

The kitten hissed and must've swiped his hand with its claws because he muttered, "Ouch! What was—"

And then the kitten jumped to the ground and stood with fur puffed out in every direction, hissing and spitting.

Leo reached up to help Felicity off the horse. She welcomed his help off the horse, but almost doubled over in pain when her feet were on the ground.

"August is out there." She motioned toward the darkness, not even knowing which direction he had gone.

"I saw him ride off to get you in the middle of the stampede."

"He saved us. Ben and me." She gasped the words more than said them. Somehow, on the back of the horse, her muscles had tightened up and now movement sent pain screaming through her ribs.

"There's not time," she said. "August saw a group of ruffians—he thought they were the same men who attacked the other wagon train. They're coming to attack us."

She saw the skeptical expression cross Coop's face, but Leo's eyes flared wide.

"Get Hollis. And Owen!" he yelled after the young man had started to run off across the circle of wagons.

She told Leo most of it, all the while taking in the camp around them.

The wagons had looked formidable and safe from the outside, but inside the camp, there were people lying near the fire with obvious injuries. Maddie was tending to a young boy, while Alice toted water from the fire to someone else. Some of the wagons were obviously battered. One listed to the side with a broken back axle.

The stampeding buffalo had caused damage. A lot of it.

And unless their company could leave behind several wagons, it meant they were stranded here until they could be repaired.

Just like the bandits wanted.

Leo repeated the most important parts of her message when Owen and Hollis appeared out of the darkness.

Obviously neither man had seen a bedroll tonight. They were alert, if visibly exhausted.

"She left him out there?" Owen burst out angrily.

Felicity choked back a sob. She hadn't wanted to

leave August—he'd insisted that this was the safest, quickest way to get the news back to the camp.

"You don't know what happened," Leo said to his brother.

Didn't they understand? There wasn't time to argue.

"Those men are coming," she said, as loudly as her burning voice would allow. "They've got guns, and they're going to come shooting."

Like a crack of lightning to punctuate her statement, a far-off shot rang out.

She glanced in the direction it had come from and saw every head nearby track that way too.

Another shot that echoed off the bluffs behind them. Then she saw a muzzle-fire.

Riders approached with heavy hoofbeats. A bullet pinged off the wood of a wagon.

"Get to cover," Hollis ordered. "Men, get your weapons."

Her warning hadn't come soon enough. They'd wasted too much time.

Ben let out a strangled sob, and Felicity put her arm around the girl, scurrying to find something to block them from what was coming.

Leo and Coop and Hollis and Owen ran in the direction the riders had fired from, then each man went flat on their bellies as they used pistols to fire back.

Screams rose as the bugle sounded and others realized what was happening. Felicity found cover behind a large barrel and huddled there, keeping Ben between her and the barrel.

"Kitty!" Ben cried out.

Oh no. The kitten had been on the ground when they'd heard the shots.

"He'll be all right." Felicity kept her arm around Ben's middle in case the girl decided to run off in search of the cat. "He probably found shelter, too."

Surely the cat would've been spooked by the noise and sudden chaos. He would hide himself around here somewhere.

"We'll find him. Later."

More shots rang through the darkness, and someone in camp cried out. Had they been hit?

Gunsmoke filled the air in choking puffs. Felicity tried to cover her mouth and nose with her hand. She couldn't see much, not hidden as she was.

Shots pinged from the other side of the circle, and there was another cry from that direction. Had the riders surrounded them? The shots seemed random, as if they came from all directions. Was there a pattern to the madness?

With the injured from the stampede, did their company have enough men to defend from every side? She didn't know.

She peeked her head out to see Leo shouting to one of his brothers, "Rifles and ammunition!"

Leo's wagon was well-stocked. She knew it. But Leo had gone to where the shots had fired and was far from his wagon now. Coop lay beneath a wagon two over from where Leo fired his gun. Two men were shooting at Coop. He was pinned.

Their revolvers only had so many shots. Six, maybe eight?

She saw Alice lean her body to shield someone near

the fire. Evangeline and Sara were crouched behind some crates near what must be their wagon.

There was no gunfire in that direction. Not yet.

Felicity let go of Ben and crawled out from behind the barrel on shaky hands and knees. She needed a better look.

It was too dangerous to cross that expanse, wasn't it? She'd seen firsthand the damage bullets could do. But Leo and Coop were protecting their entire camp. And they needed help.

August had trusted her to make the dangerous ride into camp to warn everyone. August had put his own life in danger. She could live up to his faith in her. Couldn't she?

"Come on," she said to Ben. "We're going to run over there, by Sara. You see?" She pointed. Ben nodded tearfully.

The little girl had lost her crutch back in the stampede. Felicity half picked her up and shuffle-ran until she reached Evangeline.

"Leo and Coop are pinned down. They need their rifles and more ammunition."

The other woman was crying silently, eyes wide and fearful. Felicity put her arm around her. Evangeline's father had been shot and died earlier in this dangerous journey. This must be extra terrifying for her.

"We've got to help them," Felicity said.

She thought about August and those first, far-off shots. Had those shots been his warning to the company?

He'd fought for them. Risked his life.

She could do the same.

Evangeline pointed a shaky finger at the rear of the

nearest wagon. "There's a box of ammunition inside. The rifles are underneath the wagon. I'll fetch them."

Felicity moved to the wagon, startled when something pinged and wood splintered near her shoulder.

Evangeline crouched at her feet. "Someone's shooting!"

Felicity dragged a wooden box that was heavier than Ben from the back of the wagon. She almost dropped it on her foot. Her side protested.

Evangeline appeared with two rifles in hand.

"Someone has to stay with the girls," Felicity said. "Can you do it?"

Evangeline carefully tucked the rifles in Felicity's arm. She didn't know how she'd manage to carry it all, but she had to.

"Get a rifle for yourself," Felicity told her. "Just in case."

There was no more time to think. If she thought, she'd take the coward's way out.

Felicity ducked as best she could and ran to the men.

* * *

In the starlight, August stayed low, crawling the rest of the way to the edge of the woods he'd chosen for cover. It was still dark. He thought dawn was close, but so far there was no sign of the sun lighting up the sky.

Stretched out on his belly, he pulled the rifle into position. He could see two dark shadows riding back and forth outside the circle of the wagon train. He aimed, adjusting slightly for movement, and fired. The recoil shoved his shoulder back. His ears rang from the sound.

He couldn't be sure in the dark, but he thought he'd winged the man.

A shot whined from nearby and something whizzed over his head, lodging into a tree trunk only a few feet away.

He rolled to the side and stood up, moving farther down the tree line. One of the men must've been watching for August's muzzle flash. It was too dark to see him in the woods otherwise.

On foot, it had been difficult to tail the men in the dark. He had run in the darkness, sending up prayer after prayer for Felicity's safety. The other passengers' too.

He didn't know whether she'd made it, but he'd come over the last rise and seen the white of the circled wagons in the distance. He'd only had a vague sense of where the riders must be—at an angle between him and the wagons.

He'd fired into the darkness, hoping to startle them into leaving.

But it seemed he'd only rushed their plan. Muzzle flashes lit up the darkness as they'd ridden toward the camp.

He'd heard return shots from camp. Someone was awake. Had Felicity made it back to warn them? Then more defensive shots sounded.

August ran through the night, angling for a position that would put him close enough for his rifle to do some damage but far enough away so he wouldn't be an easy target.

There'd been a lull. The shots fired from inside the circle of wagons came more sporadically. They couldn't already be out of ammunition, could they?

He'd taken a risk, stepping out of the cover of trees to fire at the nearest shadowy figure. He'd missed wide, taken two more quick shots before diving into cover when another of the men had started shooting in his direction.

And then—rapid fire from the wagon train that had the men on horseback shouting to each other.

They'd expected to surprise a sleeping, recovering camp. Instead, they'd found a worthy opponent.

But they weren't finished yet. August kept running and shooting, and now he was down to his last six bullets for the rifle. His revolver had all its shots but wouldn't do him much good at long range.

The first rays of sunlight began pouring over the horizon, giving enough light for August to see the man riding in the tree line farther to his left.

He took a shot that barely missed. The man ducked low against his horse, but he didn't ride into the woods or go back the other direction. August was still mostly hidden behind a fallen log. He steadied his rifle on top of the log, squinting against the remaining darkness and drawing a bead on the man—

"August! Behind you!" The unexpected shout was Owen's voice.

August ducked behind the log on instinct, only a scant second before a bullet splintered it.

A shot rang out from deeper in the woods. Then another. August heard a gasp of pain before the sound of hoofbeats. He lifted his head enough to see the man he'd fired at turn his horse and gallop away.

"August!"

"I'm all right!" August stayed low as he moved

through the woods to where he expected his brother to be.

Owen had his rifle stock in hand, the gun pointed toward the ground. He was alert, eyes scanning all around them.

"Am I glad to see you," August said.

More shots sounded from the prairie, toward the wagons. August ducked by reflex.

Owen motioned him to move in a westerly direction. "What in the world were you thinkin'?"

August drew up short, but under his older brother's angry glare, he kept his feet moving.

"Sending that woman back to camp? You could've been killed."

Felicity had made it. Relief battered him. He exhaled a shuddering breath.

"Is she all right? What happened in camp? They were firing back, weren't they?"

Owen shook his head. "I don't know. As soon as she said you were out here somewhere, I lit out of there to come find you."

The shots had tapered off now. Because it was light outside? The riders would be easier targets with the sun up, and the caravan had some protection in the wagons and supplies.

"I can't believe you'd put yourself at risk like this," Owen muttered. He was crashing through the brush seeming to have no compunction about all the noise he was making.

"We needed to warn the camp, and I couldn't leave the two of them out there unprotected." It was on the tip of his tongue to tell his brother about his growing feelings for Felicity. But Owen's thundercloud frown thrown over his shoulder held back August's words.

"You've got to be responsible with your choices," Owen said in full commanding mode. "You're not twelve anymore, out hunting for grouse while a horse suffers."

August fell back a step, as if he'd taken a blow to the ribs. For a second, he couldn't catch his breath.

Birdwatching.

He'd been out birdwatching instead of checking on the horses like his pa had demanded. And one of the stock horses had come down with colic and foundered. When August had come in two hours after he was supposed to, time lost exploring and birdwatching, it had been too late.

Pa had made him put the horse down himself, while Owen had watched.

August had been devastated, unable to talk about it for months afterward.

He felt an echo of that devastation right now.

Owen thought that his choice to protect Felicity over himself was like that event from his childhood? That August had acted irresponsibly?

The tips of his ears felt hot. "What would you have had me do?"

Owen must've heard the argumentative note in August's voice, the way he strove for calmness but couldn't quite get there. Owen turned and faced August squarely. The sun was coming up behind him, filtering prettily through the woods, in direct contrast to the dark expression Owen wore.

August held his rifle down at his side, his stance a mirror of his brother's.

"Anything else," Owen said, the words quiet but deadly in their intensity.

"I made the best decision I could." August matched his intensity, his protective feelings for Felicity and Ben right at the forefront.

"And there's the problem," Owen said. "What if that girl had ridden right into the murderers? Got herself killed? Who'd have come to tell us?"

His words battered August, who couldn't shake the image of Felicity overlaying what he'd seen at the massacre days ago.

He swallowed hard. "That didn't happen."

"Not this time." Another blow.

August swallowed as the image in his mind's eye twisted and changed into another memory. Of a frozen creek, broken ice, a strangled scream.

August had made wrong decisions before. And they had cost everything. He'd been trying to prove himself since Hank, since well before that. But his best was never good enough.

Who was he kidding?

Not Owen.

Owen knew the terrible cost of August's past decisions.

"I'm sorry." August didn't know if he was apologizing for today or for what had happened so long ago.

Owen's expression cleared the slightest bit. "We'll get through this. I'm here to help. I don't want to see you get yourself shot."

He clapped one hand on August's shoulder, but the heavy feeling didn't lift.

Owen was right.

What if August had put Felicity and Ben in more danger with his stupid idea? He couldn't bear it if anything happened to her.

Owen was the clear-headed one. The decisive one.

August was the one who mucked things up.

Chapter Fifteen

Rachel had been dead asleep when the first shots had fired.

She roused in her bedroll to the first screams and for a moment, thought she'd been caught in a nightmare. The screams sounded identical to those that had come when their wagon train had been attacked.

In her half-asleep state, she looked around for Evan.

Someone had lit a fire in the center of the circle of wagons and it illuminated far too many wagons and people—the company she and Evan had traveled with had been much smaller. *Wrong.*

Another scream came. Rachel jumped. Someone ran across the center of camp.

Alice.

Rachel blinked and the past fell away.

Evan was dead.

And they were under attack again.

Gunshots had been fired on the eastern part of the

circle of wagons, while she had been sleeping on the southwestern side.

She fought her way out of the bedroll, flinching at every gunshot. Her heart was pounding, and she couldn't think. Firelight flickered from a few circles whose flames hadn't fully died down overnight.

A horse whinnied. Someone cried out.

Evan had fought back when bandits with bandanas covering their faces had attacked their caravan. He'd pulled his weapon, had been killed as he'd tried to defend her and their supplies.

When she'd come out of the hiding place where Evan had sequestered her, everything had been deadly quiet. Evan was gone.

Now her instincts for protection had gone awry. She wanted to run, but without a horse, her body was too cumbersome and slow. And leaving the protection of the wagons would be a death sentence.

Where could she hide?

She was frantically looking for a place that might protect her from the flying bullets when she caught sight of Daniel. His limp was noticeable, even in the chaos and the dark.

He crouched down, sneaking toward the place where several horses had been tied off nearby. Her desire to seek safety warred with her need to check on him. Daniel hadn't been in a good place these past days, mired in his grief.

"Daniel." She hissed his name, but he kept moving.

She rushed forward a few steps, breathing hard, to catch up with him. "Daniel!"

She snagged his arm. He stopped just in front of the

horses, who were shying and dancing from the noise around them.

"It's time to go," he told her.

He smelled like a distillery, and she knew a moment of despair. Where had he found the drink?

"We can't leave the circle of wagons," she said. "We'll be shot."

As if to punctuate her statement, a shot rang out near them.

She flinched. She didn't want to stand out here in the open. "Come on."

"The only place I'm going is away from here." He pulled against her hold, but she clung tightly to him. He wasn't in his right mind, wasn't thinking clearly.

"You said you wanted to go home. Now's our chance," he growled.

"You can't run out there!" she cried.

He finally threw her off. "We ain't gonna run. We're gonna ride."

She rushed after him as he turned back to the horses. The closest one neighed, clearly spooked.

"These aren't our horses," she called out, panting as she tried to keep up.

"Doesn't matter."

He untied the rope from the closest horse, a white-faced pinto.

"What are you doing?" Her voice was high-pitched and frightened the horse into rearing.

Daniel cursed as he clung to the halter.

"You can't steal a horse," she said.

She grabbed his arm again. Between the horse

wrestling for its freedom and Rachel's hold, Daniel lost control of the horse.

He turned on her, eyes wide and angry. "Don't tell me what to do!"

He backhanded her across the face. She went reeling to the ground, catching herself on her hands and knees. Her cheek throbbed. She couldn't believe he'd struck her.

A shot rang out. A horse whinnied. The pinto had bolted. It disappeared outside the circle of wagons. From her hands and knees, she watched as Daniel untied another horse, this one a tall, black gelding.

"Don't," she breathed.

Someone shouted a warning.

She tried to get up, but the baby twisted in her belly and she cried out, knees buckling as one hand went to her stomach. She could only watch in horror as Daniel made for one of the breaks between the wagons.

Only a few yards outside the wagons, his body recoiled as if something had hit his shoulder. He fell off the horse. The animal bolted, running out into the prairie.

"No!" The word burst from her lips. She finally scrambled to her feet, stumbling a few steps toward Daniel. Was he dead?

A soft hand halted her progress. In her panicked state, it took a moment to realize Alice had come to stand beside her, was holding her back, keeping her from going to Daniel.

"They've almost run off the bandits," Alice said

gently. "Let one of the men fetch him. You've got to watch out for you and the baby."

There was something indecipherable behind her words. Alice's glance landed on Rachel's cheek, where pain still pulsed beneath the surface of her skin.

"I can hear him shouting," Alice said gently. "He's alive."

She felt numb but Alice's words made a semblance of sense. She allowed the other woman to lead her to where Evangeline sat with her little girl and Ben. Rachel allowed herself to be led to a crate like a child.

It was only when Ben brought her a handkerchief that she realized her cheeks were wet with tears.

The gunshots had stopped, she finally realized.

Felicity joined them, comforting a quietly crying Ben. She and Evangeline set about finding a quick breakfast for the girls, speaking in hushed voices about how they could help the injured from their party.

Rachel sat straight-backed as the activity went on around her. She should be helping. She knew that. But she couldn't stop shaking. She tried to hide her fisted hands in her skirts.

The baby moved again, pushing a foot or some other body part painfully into Rachel's side. She shifted, exhaled, trying to ease the discomfort.

That breath of air seemed to release something inside her. She could hear everything now. A voice nearby whispering questions about what to do if the shooters returned. Canvas flapping in the morning breeze. Angry voices saying her brother's name.

She stood up, ignoring Evangeline's soft call.

Across the circle, a group of men stood around

Daniel. She rushed to him. Daniel was sitting up, holding a bloody cloth to his shoulder. Leo and Collin stood in almost identical postures facing him.

Daniel's eyes were bloodshot. He looked rebellious, not repentant.

"He needs help." She pushed past the man on the outskirts of those watching.

Leo turned his head, eyes narrowing when he caught sight of her face.

"His wound needs tending!" Her voice rose as she registered that no one was moving to help. She pushed between two men who hadn't budged an inch, making it difficult for her pregnant body to fit between them.

Collin caught her arm before she could get any closer to Daniel. "What happened to your face?"

She clamped her lips shut. It wasn't any of his business.

"His wound—" she whimpered.

"There are others who need tending more," Leo said. His voice rang with authority and anger.

"Why don't you go help Maddie and Stella?" Collin said gently.

She tugged her arm from his grip. He let go immediately. "Daniel is my family. Why isn't anyone helping him?"

"He stole my horse." A man with a bushy black beard stepped forward. "Now the animal's run off. That's a hanging offense."

"No need to tend his wound in that case," murmured a voice from behind her.

She gasped and craned her neck, trying to see who'd said the cruel words.

"If any of you would've given us a horse, we'd have been far away from here!" Daniel bellowed.

He sounded so angry, so fierce in his blame of everyone around them.

Was this what she'd sounded like, too? Hounding every family in the wagon train as she'd tried to find a way to go back East? Her stomach sank.

She turned to Leo. Pleaded. "He isn't in his right mind. This morning brought us right back to when we were attacked—"

"He ain't been in his right mind since we met him. Been in the bottom of a bottle," said the man with the bushy beard.

Leo shook his head, his expression drawn. "He's right. You've had more warnings than we've allowed for anyone else." He directed the words at Daniel, who glared right back at him.

"He's grieving," she said.

Collin shook his head. "There's a better way to do it."

Hollis stormed over, a smear of blood on his sleeve. He didn't look injured, but his expression was fierce. "There's no time for any more squabbling. We won't help you anymore, not when you've taken advantage of everything we've done so far."

Rachel gasped. Hollis's gaze cut to her.

"Please," she begged. "You can't just kick us out." They would die in the wilderness alone. She knew it.

But Hollis's stare was hard. "You find me one person who will speak up for him," he pointed to Daniel. "One person, and we'll take the two of you to the fort like my captains promised."

She looked at the angry faces of the men circling

them. Looked past them to the closest women, one tending a fire and the other pretending not to listen.

There was no hint of compassion on any face.

What was she going to do?

* * *

The sun was rising quickly, and Felicity was growing more worried about August. Why was it taking so long for him to return? She needed to see him, wanted desperately to know he was safe.

Wanted him to hold her, tell her everything would be all right.

The tone in camp was fearful and anxious. The men had set up a double watch, and those who'd been working on repairing the wagons had redoubled their efforts. When she walked past a group of men, they spoke of being prepared when the bandits came back.

When, not if.

Some of the women were hauling water from the nearby creek, guarded by men armed with rifles. Maddie was running all over camp doctoring the handful of folks who'd been injured in the shootout as well as a couple who'd been hurt during the stampede. Evangeline was watching over Ben and Sara and some of the younger children.

Felicity couldn't haul water, and when she'd approached Leo to find out how she could best help, he'd asked her to count the ammunition left in his wagon and then seek out certain folks—he gave her a written list— and find out how much ammunition they had left. She was using her slate to keep the tally.

She tried not to think about her wagon, left out on the prairie. The oxen picketed next to it.

Fifty, fifty-two, fifty-four...

She didn't have much to lose, just a few beloved books and her dresses, and some letters she'd saved from home. She didn't want to leave them behind. But neither could she imagine asking anyone to ride out and help repair her wagon, hers and Abigail's. Not with a group of murdering bandits in the area.

She finished the count of Leo's store and was moving to the next wagon inside the circle when she heard a raspy sound.

Someone crying.

She stopped and backtracked, locating the noise in the small space between two wagons parked closely together.

Rachel sat huddled in the shadow, weeping.

Felicity glanced at the bustling activity around her. Everyone focused on their own task. No one to notice if she delayed her count for a moment.

"Are you all right?" She knelt next to Rachel, who stiffened and went silent. "Of course, you aren't. That was a silly question."

She didn't know the other woman that well, not enough to reach out and touch her or pat her shoulder. So Felicity sat on the ground next to her, within arm's distance.

"They're going to kick us out of the wagon train," Rachel said in a broken whisper, her hands covering her face.

The gossip had spread like wildfire, the news that Daniel had tried to steal a horse, that he'd been shot—

possibly by the owner of the horse he'd been on at the time—and that Hollis wanted him gone.

"Are you sure you both have to go?" Felicity asked, trying to gentle her tone.

Rachel gave a great sniffle, her voice wet when she spoke. "What do you mean?"

"Daniel has to go, but maybe Hollis would let you stay."

Rachel wiped her face with her skirt. "I have to stay with Daniel."

Felicity shook her head slightly. "Why?"

Without Rachel's hands hiding her face, Felicity could see the bruise blooming on her cheek, the skin shiny with tears. Someone had hit her, and the whispers around camp said Daniel had done it.

"He's all I have left," Rachel whispered. "Everyone else is gone."

Felicity might be making things worse, but—

"Why would you want to stay with someone who would do that..." She tipped her head and motioned to Rachel's cheek.

Rachel put her hand over the wound.

"There are decent men in this company," Felicity said. "Surely there's someone who would speak up for you. You, not Daniel."

Rachel's face crumpled.

Felicity sucked in a breath, letting her head turn and eyes wander, trying to think of a way she could comfort Rachel. She saw Owen duck through two wagons, not far away. He had a rifle in his hand and looked weary. A familiar form followed only a step behind.

August!

She wanted to run to him but was conscious of the woman beside her and the bustle of organized chaos around them.

August was scanning the camp, his eyes roving—

He caught sight of her. She felt a catch in her breath the moment their gazes collided. She thought she saw a beat of relief before he dropped his eyes. Quickly.

As if he was avoiding her stare.

She watched for a moment longer, hope rising in her throat.

He looked defeated somehow. It was there in the slump of his shoulders, the lines etched in his face. She let her gaze roam over him, searching for sign of any injury. She saw none. But he didn't glance in her direction again. Unease wriggled in her belly.

She pushed herself from the ground. She would go to him—

"Felicity?" A man's voice from nearby startled her.

Mr. Smith. "Leo said you needed to count my bullets."

His wagon was close, only a few steps from where she stood.

She couldn't refuse, shouldn't delay any longer, not with the threat of further attack hanging over their heads.

The man put the long, flat box of bullets on the tailgate of the wagon. She'd be out of sight of most of the camp.

"August!" Rachel's voice, from not far away. It brought Felicity's head up.

"I need to—I need to talk to you." Anybody could hear the broken sentence, the tears in her voice.

Felicity put her head down and tried to focus on

counting bullets, but she had to start all over when she realized Rachel had pulled August outside of the ring of wagons—only a few feet away from Felicity, easily within earshot. Neither could see her, but she could hear everything they said.

"I need help." Rachel's voice held a pleading note.

It was far too easy for Felicity to picture her beautiful, tear-stained face. Even in grief, Rachel was incredibly beautiful.

"What is it?" August sounded calm and steady, his usual manner. And then a little anger seeped through when he added, "What happened to your face?"

Rachel told him of Daniel's bad choice, calling it a mistake made by a grieving man.

August only listened.

"Hollis said—" Rachel couldn't seem to get the words out.

Felicity went back to counting, striving for focus.

"He said that Daniel can't stay in the wagon train unless someone will stand up for him. Can you—can speak on his behalf?"

Felicity's imagination was too good. She could easily picture August embracing the weeping Rachel. He had a kind heart. He couldn't stand by while Rachel cried as if her heart was breaking.

"I can't do that," he said gently. "He's made his own mistakes."

At the muffled sound of her sobbing, Felicity knew a terrible jealousy as she imagined Rachel's head buried in his chest.

And then a loud, shaky inhale. "Then I have another question. I can't—I'm frightened over what could happen to me and the baby. If I had a husband to walk by my side, things might be all right."

Felicity's heart began pounding in her ears. Husband? What was Rachel saying? She'd suggested to Rachel that she find a decent man, a decent family to stand up for her. But she hadn't meant August.

"We're friends, aren't we? We get along all right."

Felicity's face went hot, her extremities cold. She gripped the wagon bed, her eyes not seeing anything in front of her.

"I need a husband," Rachel said. "It might as well be a friend."

Felicity felt the bottom drop out of her stomach.

Rachel was asking August to marry her.

August, who'd come to her rescue once before. Felicity's mind flipped through every person he'd helped.

He was a rescuer.

But she still willed him to say no. To say that he had feelings for someone else—her.

But he didn't say that.

What he said was, "I need to speak to Owen."

Chapter Sixteen

August found his brother just finishing a conversation with Leo. It was only midmorning, but he was exhausted from little sleep. Every step felt like trudging through molasses.

"I need to talk to you," August said.

Owen nodded toward a wagon listing badly to one side. "Leo asked us to help get the axle repaired on this wagon. We need to be ready to roll out."

August was reminded of Felicity's wagon and oxen, still vulnerable out in the open. The only saving grace might be that it was slightly hidden in that low spot in the valley. He wished he would have thought to take off the canvas so the wagon would be harder to spot.

Thinking about Felicity made the dull ache in his chest turn to a roar. He forced it down, forced his focus away.

"We can't outrun them." August fell in step with his brother.

With the slower oxen pulling the wagons, there was no speed advantage over single men on horseback.

"I know," Owen said, distracted. "But the fort is less than ten days away. If we can make it there, we'll have some protection."

Did they have enough ammunition to hold them until then? What if more travelers got injured, got shot?

August didn't like it one bit. But he held his tongue as Owen greeted Horace Rollins and his eighteen-year-old son, Jude, who were anxiously taking off the wagon wheel in front of the broken axle. When they needed the wagon bed lifted, August stepped into place shoulder-to-shoulder with his brother.

"Did you hear about Daniel?" he barely breathed the words.

Will you marry me? Rachel's question swirled his belly. All he could think about was Felicity. About her in his arms, the fierce sweetness of her kiss when they'd parted last.

He wanted Felicity. But Owen's words rang in his head, too.

You've got to be responsible with your choices. You're not twelve anymore.

August didn't have a track record of making good decisions.

He needed Owen to weigh in.

"I heard." Owen was tight-lipped.

"Rachel has a big bruise on her cheek." It made August angry that anyone would hurt a woman. Daniel didn't deserve any leniency, as far as August was concerned. But that left Rachel in a dire situation.

"Would Hollis really kick her out of the wagon train too?"

Hollis was fair, but tough.

A muscle was ticking in Owen's cheek. "Hollis wants her to stop causing trouble."

"Should I marry her then?" The words tasted like ash in August's mouth.

No.

The answer came strong and loud inside him.

Owen considered for a moment. "You two get along."

She'd said the same thing. They were friends. But he felt more than friendship for Felicity.

He was falling in love with her.

"I told you before that if you really intend to honor our wager, you should consider her."

Was that his answer then? Owen had thought they were a match all this time?

Someone spoke to Owen from his other side and August was left to stew in his thoughts.

Owen thought he should marry Rachel.

Rachel needed help.

But August's heart wanted something different.

He tried to ignore his turmoil throughout the day. Tempers grew short as afternoon turned into evening. Five of their men had been injured. Two children and one woman had been bruised and battered when the buffalo stampeded.

Most of the wagons had been repaired, but they couldn't travel at night. And people feared another attack. Folks gathered around a few cookfires, anxious and worried as they tried to eat supper.

August was assigned first watch. He pulled away to

the outside of the wagon circle under the pretense of checking over his rifle. He wanted to be alone.

He didn't get his wish.

Soft footsteps rustled the grass behind him. He braced himself to tell Rachel he didn't have an answer yet, but when he turned, it was Felicity who stood in the fading sunlight. She held the edge of a wagon, as if she hadn't quite decided whether she was coming after him or not.

His heart did an awful kind of flip, happy to see her and broken at the same time.

"I just wanted to check on you," she whispered. He saw the hesitation in her stance.

"I'm fine." His words sounded abrupt, and she blinked. He turned his face so he wouldn't see if his curt tone had hurt her. "Not a scratch on me."

There was so much more he wanted to say. It was all bottled inside, making his chest ache. He looked at her again. "What about you? Ribs?"

She made a dismissing motion with her hand, but he saw the way she stood gingerly, carefully taking each breath, making each movement.

He wanted to hold her, to check for himself that she was whole and healthy.

But he didn't have that right. Not if he was going to go through with marrying Rachel.

He turned away and knocked his hat off, running his empty hand through his hair while he clutched the stock of his rifle so tightly that he thought it might bend.

"I owe you an explanation," he said roughly.

She was silent for so long that he thought maybe

she'd left, but when he half-turned, she was still standing there, her eyes shadowed.

"You don't owe me anything." There was a quiet acceptance in her voice. He didn't understand it. He didn't accept any of this.

"I was nine when I killed my ma."

He hadn't meant to blurt it out like that, the words falling like stones, each one causing a ripple that should rend the very air around them.

He felt her freeze, sensed that she'd stopped breathing.

"She was pregnant. As far along as Rachel—maybe more. It was the dead of winter."

The words wouldn't stop now, unleashed by his pain, uncorked by the first admission. He stared at the place where the setting sun gilded the horizon gold.

"Pa came in from chores that morning with a bad fever—he was delirious by lunchtime. That was about when Ma went into labor." He stared at the setting sun, the pain of it burning into his eyes. It was far less than what he deserved.

"She begged Owen to take her to the neighbor's place. She was in a lot of pain and right scared of bringing that baby into the world all by herself."

He could still feel the fear emanating from her as she sat on the edge of the bed in his room, trying to stay away from Pa and his fever.

"Owen refused?"

He didn't realize he'd gone silent until her soft question brought him back into the present. He shook his head.

"It was snowing, and a fair distance to the neighbors'

house. Owen claimed Pa had told him we needed to stay home." August still didn't know if that was true or if Owen had needed to believe it was.

"She begged me, crying, gasping in pain every few minutes. She was my ma." He couldn't refuse her, not when she'd pled with him for help.

"I got the horses hitched to the wagon box, fitted with sleigh runners." His hands had been half-frozen by the time he'd accomplished it. "We started out all right, but part of our trail to the neighbors' place ran right alongside a deep fork of the nearby river. It was frozen over—"

But not all the way through.

"I did my best to steer through the snow, but the sleigh runner got onto the ice. It cracked and then broke."

Everything had happened so fast after that. The horses had bolted, saving the sleigh, but Ma had been jostled out of the side.

August could still remember the terror of watching her fall into the dark, icy water.

"I couldn't drag her out." His voice was ragged as he admitted to it. She'd been taller than Rachel, heavy with child, and her dress and coat and shoes weighted with the water. She'd been so weak from the labor...

He hadn't been able to save her.

"It was my decision to drive her," he said when the pain became too great, when he had to snap out of the memory or start howling. He needed her to know why he couldn't trust himself, why he was deferring to Owen's judgment now.

She watched him with big, tear-filled eyes. He hadn't realized she was crying until now. Felicity had such a tender heart.

She clung to the edge of that wagon and all he wanted to do was draw her into his arms.

Still making the wrong decision.

But he stopped himself from stepping toward her. Barely.

"I have to do the right thing now," he said, the words cutting his throat like glass.

She didn't say a word. Just nodded. And ducked back inside the safety of the circle of wagons.

He wiped his own tears away with his sleeves. Somehow, he had to find the courage to stand guard tonight.

* * *

Felicity lay awake inside the tent, though it had been hours since she and Ben had turned in. The girl's even breathing created a soft cadence in the enclosed space.

Abigail had never come to bed; perhaps she was still tending the wounded.

Felicity should be tired. Her body was exhausted. It was her brain that wouldn't quiet.

She lay flat on her back and slowly stretched her hand out over her head. A feather-soft touch batted at her fingertips. Once, and then again.

The kitten. August's kitten. Ben kept it, fed it, and watched over it, but any time the kitten saw August, it darted straight toward him.

Like she wanted to do.

She closed her eyes against the pain in her heart.

The kitten tapped her fingers again. She tilted her head, slowly so as not to wake Ben. The kitten took that as an invitation to play and promptly laid its body down next to Felicity's arm and began to paw at her hair, coming loose from its braid.

Afraid that the kitten would wake Ben, she gently scooped it into her hands and tucked it against her chest before she got up and left the tent.

It had cooled in the night. She grabbed her shawl just before the tent flap closed behind her. And then she saw Abigail. Not tending the wounded. Sitting wrapped in a blanket, near the fading fire.

It hit Felicity with a sudden force that she didn't want to be alone. She took the kitten and went to sit near her friend.

Abigail looked up from the fire. "Can't sleep?"

Felicity nodded. "I thought Ben would be too frightened to go to sleep, but it's me that can't seem to keep my eyes closed."

Abigail took a long stick and stirred the fire.

Felicity used a string from her shawl to keep the kitten occupied in her lap. She let her eyes wander, taking in just how quiet and still the camp was. No movement.

No—

Wait. There *was* movement. Outside the circle of wagons more guards than she'd ever seen patrolled in the dark.

She didn't want to think about what could happen if they were attacked again, so she jerked her focus back inside the wagons. If only it hadn't strayed to Owen and August's wagon, not far away. Another fire glowed near their tent; a figure tucked in a bedroll sleeping near the warmth. Blonde hair spilled out of the top of the bedroll.

Rachel.

Heart breaking all over again, Felicity turned her head in the opposite direction and pressed her cheek on her shoulder. Tears pricked her eyes and even though she squeezed them closed, the tears fell free.

She hadn't been able to keep August from her mind for snatches of more than a few minutes. She couldn't stop thinking about the little boy he'd been, trying to help and then save his mother. She'd seen the devastation in his face, a grown man now, but still that broken little boy inside. She'd wanted to hold him, to wrap her arms around him and press close, take his hurts from him.

But she'd also been aware of how he held himself carefully distant.

I have to do the right thing.

She understood now. It made sense that he'd grown up into the man who rescued those in need, even at the cost of lost sleep, injury, his emotions...

August was trying to right the wrongs of the past in his own way. He'd made the decision to marry Rachel; she'd seen it in his resigned, determined expression.

How could Felicity ask him to choose her now? The words simply wouldn't come. She would never tell him— or anyone—how deeply she'd grown to care for him.

Was this love? This feeling of being rent in two, unable to breathe for the ache of losing him, not wanting to eat or sleep? She wiped her cheek on her shoulder and tried to even out her breathing. She should've learned her lesson long ago.

A man strode past, eyes and ears alert as he moved from his tent toward the darkness outside.

Leo.

He registered her and Abigail sitting beside the fire and made a detour.

"You two all right?" he asked.

Felicity couldn't find words, but Abigail nodded. "As much as we can be, I suppose."

Felicity ached so badly within that she'd only given passing thought to the danger still lurking outside their camp.

Leo's gaze encompassed her briefly. "It's been a busy evening. I haven't had a chance to thank you, until now."

Thank her?

"Running ammunition to me and my brothers helped hold off those murdering thieves. I was on my last shot when you brought more bullets."

His praise sent a faint warmth through her. It wasn't enough to touch the icy shards of her heart, but his kindness mattered. He tipped his hat and strode off into the darkness, leaving them both staring at the fire.

"I watched you," Abigail said suddenly. "I was hiding inside the wagon, too scared to move. There's a little tear in the canvas. I could see everything."

Poor Abigail. What had happened this morning was terrifying. She'd been right to hide.

"You were so brave," Abigail said, her focus on the fire. "Running back and forth like you did, taking bullets to the men."

There was perhaps a hint of admiration in her voice, but Felicity shook her head. The kitten had grown sleepy and now curled in the crook of Felicity's arm. She stroked its back with two fingertips. "I didn't do anything special," she murmured.

"Yes, you did," Abigail argued. "Most of the woman were cowering in fear, but not you."

Felicity shook her head. "Maybe it isn't something to be proud of."

A log from the fire cracked, sending sparks up toward the sky.

"Perhaps there is something broken inside me," she whispered, the words resonating. "I've had to keep my emotions separate from the tasks at hand for so long. Even if I was tired and overwrought, I could make supper for my younger siblings."

Abigail scrunched her nose up. "Have you always been so?"

Felicity began to shrug but then thought better of it. "I... don't know. When I was very young, my stepmother didn't favor me."

She hadn't thought about those early days in a very long time. Maybe it was the way her feelings for August had cracked her chest open, but all of a sudden, those feelings from when she'd been all of four years old slammed into her with breathless intensity.

Celia had never given her affection. Felicity had tried to climb into her lap once or twice and been pushed away. She didn't sing like Mama had. She never smiled, not at Felicity.

"I was almost five when my stepsister was born," she told Abigail now. "And my stepmother needed extra rest for months afterward. One afternoon, the baby was crying, and I felt so sorry for her. I went and played peek-a-boo with her in the cradle. She quieted. I don't know how long we played. And when I looked up, my stepmother was there. She smiled at me for the first time... maybe ever."

She didn't know where the words were coming from. She never spoke of this. Maybe the events of the day truly had broken something inside her because more words tumbled out.

"Soon I was changing diapers and feeding the baby and fetching eggs... Celia was always happy with me when I was helpful." Felicity had been so starved for affection, for any sign that she was wanted, loved. "So I worked. As hard as I could. All the time. Put my own feelings aside. Even when I was sick with a fever and aches..."

Abigail shook her head. "It isn't right to work a child like that."

Felicity knew that now. She'd left home at sixteen, when Celia had been expecting her seventh child. Late one night, she'd cleaned up after supper, washed laundry, and put up a loaf of dough for bread for the morning. She was almost sleeping on her feet when she'd overheard her father and stepmother talking in low tones from their bedroom on the first floor.

Father had asked whether Norah should be taking on some chores now that she was graduating the sixth grade. Celia had answered that Felicity could handle everything just fine on her own. There had been no love in her voice. No appreciation. Only expectation.

Felicity understood as quickly as the strike of a lightning bolt. Celia was never going to love her, not even if she worked her fingers to the bone. She'd give Felicity more and more work to do, while she doted on her blood children.

Felicity had known then that she was the only one who would look out for her own interests. She'd left home the next morning, with only a few dollars of egg money in her pocket.

She was so lost on her thoughts of those times, almost a decade ago now, that she didn't realize Ben had crept from the tent. Tears streaked the little girl's cheeks. She came right to Felicity, who opened her shawl. Ben climbed into her lap, dislodging the kitten.

Abigail looked on, her gaze considering. "I'm sorry," she said quietly. "For not understanding when you tried to tell me why it was important that you earn your way."

Another small warmth infused Felicity. Abigail had been a friend on this journey when Felicity had desperately needed one. "I'm sorry, too."

They shared a small smile.

Ben sighed into Felicity's shoulder and dozed back into sleep.

Felicity looked down at the curve of the girl's cheek, her expression peaceful in sleep.

Ben needed her. It didn't matter that August hadn't chosen her. Ben had. She would find a way to protect and care for them both.

If they survived the next few days.

Chapter Seventeen

Felicity had woken abruptly to someone shaking her shoulder.

It was still night, too early for dawn. She realized she'd fallen asleep next to the fire; it was now doused. Everything was dark. But it wasn't quiet.

"We're pulling out." That sounded like Alice, but the voice was disembodied in the darkness and Felicity was already disoriented.

Ben stirred. Felicity heard a soft meow and gripped the girl's arm. "Keep the kitten close," she warned.

"No light," said Alice quickly. "Women will be driving the wagons, all children inside them. Anybody that can ride and shoot is on horseback. Leo said for you and Abigail and Ben to drive Collin's wagon."

Collin's wife, Stella, and her two younger sisters could ride, so that made sense.

Felicity found the wagon in the dark and boosted Ben and the kitten inside it, with whispered instructions not to move an inch. She and Abigail hurriedly broke down the tent and stowed it in the wagon with Ben.

"I'm hungry!" Ben whined in a whisper, her voice carrying in the darkness.

"Shh," Abigail cautioned her.

"We'll get breakfast soon enough," Felicity said, though she didn't know when.

Before she'd dropped off to sleep in front of the fire, she'd seen Leo return, watched him visit a couple of the tents and squat down outside, speaking quietly.

This must've been Hollis's plan—to get the caravan away before the men who'd attacked could come back.

A tall form appeared out of the darkness, and Felicity gasped. Too late, she realized it was Collin, leading the oxen.

"All right?" he whispered.

She shook her head even though he couldn't see her in the dark. She helped him hitch the oxen into their braces, her fingers trembling in the damp cool of morning.

There was no bugle to herald their departure, only silent footsteps hurrying about the camp, making sure nothing was forgotten. She had clambered up into the wagon seat, her ribs aching when she had to pull herself up. Abigail was whispering to Ben in the back of the wagon. Felicity could hear whimpers from the little girl. She was probably frightened.

So was Felicity.

Maybe they hadn't hurried fast enough because silver light began slipping over the Eastern horizon.

A whisper carried down the line that the lead wagon was pulling out. She heard murmurs from the wagon closest in front of her and realized by squinting in the near dark that August was helping Rachel into the wagon seat.

Felicity cut her eyes away, though her mind filled with the image of his gentle hands boosting the beautiful woman into the seat. Maybe he'd place a hand on her knee in comfort.

Felicity's stomach knotted tighter.

Another tall form came out of the darkness, followed not far behind by a man stumbling—she realized only at the last second that the second man was Daniel. His hands were tied in front of him.

"You're gonna leave me out in the open to get shot again?" Daniel's plaintive whine was like a fly buzzing in her ears.

"Shut up." That was Owen, his tone menacing. He was tying the rope that secured Daniel's hands to the back of the wagon Rachel now drove.

"You make one wrong move and I'll be the one that shoots you," Owen warned.

He'd barely stopped talking when the wagon started rolling. Owen stepped clear and then took one glance at Felicity before he darted in front of the oxen and swung up into his saddle. August was already seated on his horse only a few feet beyond. The two men moved almost identically as they took their rifles out of the sheaths on their saddles and held them at the ready.

Owen moved up the line, while August rode along-side Rachel's wagon. Felicity could see his strong back and the horse's rump as she flicked the reins and her oxen started moving.

She'd only driven the wagon once since her injury

and the tension of holding the reins pulled at her ribs. She was still sore from yesterday. But she ignored it, focusing on what was in front of her.

The wagons were setting a fast clip, but she knew it would still be several minutes before the wagons that had been circled in line behind her were rolling, too. The sky had barely lightened, and she was focused on keeping her wagon in line with Rachel's.

She saw Daniel try and heft himself onto the back of the wagon. It didn't work. He stumbled and went to his knees to be dragged for a moment before he caught the tailgate with one hand and pulled himself up. He was cursing and yelling, fighting with the rope that bound him.

A shot rang out from somewhere at the rear of the wagon train.

The hair on Felicity's arms rose, fear stole her breath.

Another shot, then two answering.

August wheeled his horse and passed by her wagon in a matter of seconds.

"Felicity!" Ben's voice rang out from inside the wagon, terror obvious in her tone.

"It's all right," she called back, but she didn't know whether that was true.

More shots. Shouting, from far off.

And then August was back, glancing at her for only a moment. "Keep going," he called out from his horse. "Faster!"

He nudged his horse into a gallop. She saw him shout to Rachel, then disappear up front.

More men came riding beside them. Cowboys she recognized, ones who usually watched the herd of cattle traveling with them. And they'd left the herd to help defend the wagons at the back?

Shots fired in a quick cadence. They couldn't outrun men on horseback, could they?

"Felicity!" Ben's wail got louder from inside the wagon.

"Ben! Stop! Sit back down!" Abigail's muffled voice from inside sounded fearful and then frantic.

Suddenly, Ben tumbled into the seat beside Felicity. She reached out a hand to secure the girl from spilling onto the ground. At this fast pace, she'd be gravely injured.

Ben clung to Felicity's middle; her ribs panged but she ignored it as she tried to keep her focus on the oxen.

"Circle up!" came the call from a nearby cowboy.

Rachel's wagon began slowly turning back to the south.

More shots. More shouts.

Daniel was still struggling with the rope. Felicity saw it snap where he was connected to the wagon. For a moment, she thought the change in velocity would send him to the ground—she was far too close and wouldn't be able to stop the oxen, not with a heavy wagon behind them.

And then he jumped and caught the top of the tailgate with his still-bound hands. In a matter of seconds, he'd crawled up and over and gone inside.

There were no cowboys in sight; they'd gone behind her wagon. She was still moving fast, turning, to try and look behind her for help.

"Rachel!" she screamed. "Watch out!"

Suddenly, a cowboy appeared from behind her wagon, riding close on her right side.

She didn't recognize his handlebar mustache and scruffy appearance.

The wagons were slowing now, shots still peppering the air from behind her.

Daniel must have knocked loose the tie securing the canvas at the back of Rachel's wagon, because it flapped open. Felicity had a clear view of him crawling up to Rachel.

Felicity screamed her friend's name again. From the corner of her eye, she saw a rider approaching from behind, on the left.

Daniel and Rachel struggled on the driver's seat. Felicity's breath strangled in her chest. He wouldn't hurt his pregnant sister, would he?

And then Rachel tumbled off the wagon seat, landing hard on the ground.

Felicity registered August on horseback, almost even with her as she tried to stop the oxen before they ran right over Rachel.

Daniel was now in control of the wagon. It careened out of line and off to the right.

The cowboy still keeping pace with Felicity suddenly loomed over her.

Ben screamed as the cowboy tugged them both forcefully from the wagon seat and onto his horse, Ben squashed between her body and the cowboy's.

Felicity struggled, panicking. No one was driving that wagon. And Abigail was still in the back.

For a split second everything seemed to go still. August had come out of his saddle in mid-stride and now stood over Rachel. But he was looking straight at Felicity, at the man who'd grabbed her, with stark fear on his face.

This wasn't one of their cowboys. Felicity hadn't known this man. He must be one of their attackers.

She saw the struggle in August's face.

And then the decision as he knelt over Rachel.

Then the frozen moment was broken as the wagon passed between them, out of control, and the pair disappeared from sight.

August was four wagons back when he saw Daniel break free. He'd spurred his horse into a gallop by the time Daniel had climbed into the wagon.

He'd been aware of Felicity since the moment he'd woken. He couldn't bear to look at her. It hurt too much. But that hadn't kept him from knowing where she was at every moment.

He knew she was in the wagon behind Rachel's and couldn't help sneaking a glance at her in the wagon seat as he passed by.

She was holding on to Ben, who clung to her like a lifeline.

Rachel shrieked when Daniel overtook her at the front of the wagon. He heard it over the pounding hooves and gunshots.

Rachel needed help.

He saw Daniel overpower her, saw Rachel hit the ground on her side, her head bouncing in a way that made his stomach turn.

Someone shouted from horseback nearby, the sound audible amidst the ring of gunshots.

He pulled his leg over the saddle and his feet hit the ground before his horse had pulled up.

Daniel was stealing the wagon; it wobbled badly as he pulled out of the circling wagons.

Then August became aware of a struggle at Felicity's wagon. He looked up just as a man he didn't recognize, a man riding a blue roan, jerked her out of the wagon and onto his horse, taking Ben with her.

August knew a moment of frozen fear.

Rachel lay at his feet, wagons traveling dangerously fast and right at them.

Felicity had just been ousted from her wagon by an unknown assailant.

There was no time for conscious thought. How could he choose the life of one woman over another?

He registered the terror on Felicity's face for a split-second before he bent to scoop up Rachel.

She was limp and heavy in his arms. He stumbled one step and was nearly plowed down by the oxen from Felicity's wagon—now without a driver. He saw Abigail struggling to get into the seat, to grab the reins.

His heart was pounding as he looked for Felicity. There—

The rider was racing off across the prairie.

"Owen!" he bellowed. But his brother was riding after Daniel and the wagon veering outside the circle.

August went to his horse, Rachel still in his arms. He was peripherally aware of Abigail regaining control of the oxen, the wagon slipping into place in the circle and rolling to a stop. He changed course and ran toward Abigail.

Rachel roused, gasping in pain, her arms clinging to his shoulders.

"You all right? The baby?"

"I don't know," she responded in a tearful gasp.

"Abigail!" He shouted over the shots.

Abigail set the brake and jumped down. "He took Felicity and Ben! Just ripped right off the wagon seat!"

August set Rachel on her feet near the back of the wagon, careful to stay out of the way of the next nearest wagon, driven by a sobbing woman, rolling to a hard stop.

Through the break in the wagons, he and Rachel both had a clear view of Owen overtaking Daniel's wagon. Owen was shouting. Daniel seemed to ignore him. And then two riders closed in on them, bandanas over the lower half of their faces and pistols drawn.

Owen raised his rifle and took at shot at one; the other man fired, and Owen shot again.

The wagon careened to the side and August couldn't see any more. Had Daniel lost control?

"Take care of her," August ordered Abigail.

He ran to his horse and jumped into the saddle, the horse moving before he'd gotten his feet in the stirrups.

Daniel's wagon had stopped; Owen used it for cover as he tried to fend off the two gunmen trying to circle him.

August raised his rifle and took aim, catching one of the men in the shoulder.

Owen looked back at him, then leaned into the wagon seat. What was he doing?

August kept riding, taking another shot at the first rider.

"Where's Felicity?" he shouted to his brother.

Owen hauled Daniel onto his saddle, face down in his lap. Blood dripped from the man's hand onto the ground.

Not good.

August scanned the prairie but the rider who'd carted off Felicity had disappeared.

A bullet whizzed by August's shoulder. A near miss.

"Get back to the wagons!" Owen screamed. He cantered toward August and the wagons.

August wheeled his horse as more shots sizzled by, too close for comfort.

There was no shelter here, only the lone wagon out in the prairie.

And Felicity was gone.

He couldn't chase after her without looking for tracks or evidence, and couldn't go slow enough to see that, not while the wagons were under attack and men were shooting at him.

Anger and fear released from his chest in a frustrated shout as his horse cleared the two wagons. He pulled up quickly, but there was no respite from the shooting, now aimed right where he and Owen had flown into the safety of the wagons.

"Where's Felicity?" Abigail cried. She knelt on the ground near Rachel, who was pale and had one hand cradling her belly.

He shook his head.

Owen had come to a stop not far away and now bodily removed Daniel from the saddle. There was blood everywhere, and the man was too still. A small stain on the left side of Owen's shoulder bloomed dark red. Had Owen been hit? He wasn't acting like it, but that didn't look like Daniel's blood, either.

August knew the bad news before his brother looked straight at him and shook his head. Daniel was dead.

Shots pinged too close to the women. August sidled behind the nearest wagon and returned fire, but his mind was elsewhere.

Felicity.

He had no idea why she'd been taken. No idea where the bandit had taken her. The river cut through the southern end of this prairie pasture. It was flat straight to the West. Where could he have gone?

"August, I need your head on straight," Owen called out, now on foot and taking up a firing position two wagons over.

Did Owen even know that Felicity had been taken—and by a guy who'd probably just as soon kill her as look at her? That August's heart was somewhere out there with her?

August felt darkness start to pull him under.

Chapter Eighteen

Later, August couldn't have said how he'd come to be lying on his belly beneath one of the wagons—not his, because the wagon that belonged to him and Owen was still out in the wide open where Daniel had left it.

When he came to himself, he realized his rifle chamber was empty. Had he taken a shot? Two?

There were three men on horseback, circling just out of rifle range. Shots echoed from the opposite side of the wagon train, somewhere behind August.

Someone was crying.

He turned his head over his shoulder and saw Rachel lying over Daniel's unmoving body, sobbing. His focus snapped back into place; he'd been seeing things through a murky pond, everything muffled and a little distorted.

Felicity was missing. Someone had taken her.

And August was trapped inside this circle of wagons.

The murdering thieves who were out there shooting

at them would have a much easier target if he rode out alone on a horse.

He lay frozen in indecision, fear swamping him. Visions of his mother disappearing under that dark, frozen creek water flitted through his mind. Then a vision of Felicity lying on the ground, shot like the people from that massacred wagon train.

What if he was already too late?

Why hadn't he moved faster?

"Owen!" he bellowed.

Coop startled. August hadn't realized the man was underneath the wagon next to him. The man took a lazy shot with a rifle in the direction of the nearest rider, a tall man in a black duster. He glanced at August and then went back to reloading his gun.

August rolled free of the wagon and sat up—still conscious that he needed to stay low. He found his brother behind the wagon wheel of a nearby wagon, reloading his revolver.

"We have to go after Felicity and Ben," August called to his brother.

Owen shook his head. He had a bullet between his teeth and barely glanced up. He was favoring his left arm.

Maybe he didn't know what had happened.

"One of the attackers rode up and pulled both of them right out of the wagon seat." The words spilled out of him, tumbling over each other in his haste.

Owen shook his head again. "They're targeting the eastern side of the wagon train. Frank Teller's been hit and they're getting closer each time they ride up. We've got to protect the people here."

Owen's matter-of-fact manner said his decision had already been made. Or maybe he was acting on Hollis's orders. Was Owen simply fulfilling his duty?

Protect the people here.

But Felicity was a traveler too, and his mind showed him the possibility of her gruesome death all over again.

"Felicity needs help," he said. "We can't let them kill her like they did those others."

Owen shook his head again, frowning. "It's too dangerous. We stay here."

And that was that.

"We'll go after her when we've fought these off."

Owen was gone, heading at a dead run toward where the shots were firing on the other side of the wagons.

"Get your gun loaded. I need your sharpshooter skills!" He called the words over his shoulder. August was left to obey.

But he was frozen on his tookus, his chest cinched so tight he couldn't breathe.

Owen wanted to stay here; he was willing to risk Felicity's life, and Ben's, to save the majority.

What if the bandits kept them trapped all day? What if they couldn't fight them off?

Felicity would be left with the thieving murderers who would do terrible things to her. Maybe kill her.

A shot cracked from only feet away. Coop, still lazily firing, held off the three men keeping them trapped on this side of the circle. "You'd best hurry up. Get that rifle loaded."

August pressed his palm flat against his chest, where he felt the cutting pain. He still couldn't breathe.

Coop's words finally registered. August didn't move

but to turn his head. Coop wasn't even looking at him. He was sighting his rifle again, moving the barrel just slightly as he followed the movement of one of the men out there.

"Go on," he said now, his tone casual, like they were at a tea party or something. "Your brother handed out orders."

"Shut up," August said. He couldn't think. He couldn't remember which direction the bandit had taken Felicity. Everything had happened so quickly. Those fractured moments were a blur in his memory.

Coop spoke as if he hadn't heard. "Everybody on this wagon train knows you follow orders real good."

A flare of anger roared through August. He wanted to sock the other man in the face, but he wasn't within striking distance.

Coop fired again. "Got one. In the arm." He began to reload, his movements quick and efficient. "I heard you tell Hollis we needed to move the wagons out of range of the buffalo. Also heard Owen overrule you. And look what happened."

August had put that out of his mind in the events of the past seventy-two hours. It was true, though. He'd wanted to travel in a different direction, more northerly, away from the river.

Would the buffalo have been able to stampede and disrupt their travel if Owen and Hollis had listened to him?

He didn't owe Coop any explanation, but he found himself saying, "I don't always make the best decisions."

Coop's lips twisted in a derisive smile. Was it self-directed? He fired a quick shot, then began reloading again. "Seems like Owen and Hollis don't either. Hollis drove us right into that twister. And that woman sobbing over there might argue that your brother got her brother killed."

It was a twist on the truth. Daniel had done some unforgivable things. He'd hit Rachel. He'd wrestled her out of that wagon. But had he deserved to die? August couldn't say.

Owen had been the one to tie him to that wagon in the first place.

Coop's argument made a warped kind of sense. Were Owen's decisions really any better than August's?

August had decided to obey Ma all those years ago, and he'd been living with the consequences of his choices ever since. But Ma had been certain she couldn't deliver that baby on her own with two young sons as her only help. If August had chosen differently, if he'd refused to help her, would she have been right? What if there had been complications and she died anyway? Would Owen have still blamed him? Would that have been his fault?

Every decision had consequences. Logically, he knew that. And he'd been carrying the weight of decisions made so long ago, believing he couldn't be trusted to make a good decision.

But what about the night he'd found Felicity trapped in that demolished wagon? He'd followed a gut instinct to locate her. Same thing when he'd found Hollis suffering from a dangerous head injury. Owen had told him that continuing to look for the wagon master was fruitless, but Hollis had been alive. If they'd left him out in the wilderness, helpless and injured, he'd be dead by now.

August couldn't know what consequences would come from each decision he made. But he knew he couldn't let Owen be the one to make his decisions any longer. Owen had a lot of responsibilities, and he liked it that way. He enjoyed being in charge and ordering people around. But he didn't know everything.

He didn't know how desperately August loved Felicity. That a part of him would die if she did.

He had to go after her, rescue her. That was his decision.

He looked over at Coop. "I need some help. You wanna do something stupid?"

Coop grinned.

* * *

Felicity struggled against the assailant holding her on the horse's back. He'd gotten one arm around her, but her hands were free so she clawed at his face, though it twisted her ribs at this awkward angle.

He cursed and hit her temple with his fist. The blow sent her spinning into darkness.

She roused to the motion of a horse underneath her; she'd been arranged so she was lying on her stomach over the horse's back and the motion and the fact that her head hung low made her feel queasy. She could feel Ben patting her shoulder; trying to wake her up?

She refused to be killed. Or let anything happen to Ben.

Feeling so nauseated it took everything in her to

attempt to sit up, she balled her fist, determined to hit her assailant.

But she only moved a few inches when she heard a pistol being cocked.

"I don't want to shoot you, but I will."

She froze.

Several things happened at once.

The man slowed his horse.

Ben said, "Pa, don't shoot Felicity!"

She went off balance, shifted when the horse started slowly down an incline.

Pa?

Ben's words registered as the horse stopped with its front feet angled down a steep hill.

"I'm gonna help you down. You run off and I'll shoot you."

She shied away when he moved to touch her, instead sliding off backwards. Her feet hit the ground with a jarring thud and her aching head put her off balance. She stumbled backwards, right into a patch of plum trees. The dwarf trees had spikes instead of branches and she gasped. She tried to untangle herself but managed to get scratches up and down her arms and across her cheek before she got out.

The man had dismounted and was helping Ben off. He held his gun loosely in his right hand, not pointed at her but still a threat.

Ben clung to his leg the moment she was on the ground. "Pa, I knew you was alive!"

Felicity felt reality shift as she watched the little girl cry with her face pressed against her father's leg. The man put his hand tenderly on top of Ben's head.

Ben was the daughter of one of the killers?

"Let me go," Felicity said as she took a shuffling step away from the man and his horse, keeping clear of the bramble of plum trees.

"I said if you run off, I'd shoot you," he growled.

She couldn't reconcile Ben, the sweet and precocious girl, with this man who threatened her.

"Siddown," he ordered. He set Ben back from him and spoke to her. "Can you get my rope from the saddle?"

She nodded, beaming at him, and went to the horse.

He waved his gun at Felicity. "Scoot back. All the way to that bush."

She shook her head, but when he aimed the revolver at her, she had no choice. She shuffled backward awkwardly until she felt the plum tree trunk, it's spiky branches brushing at her hair.

"Put your arms together behind the tree. Hand it to me," his first command was directed at Felicity, the second to Ben.

Felicity had to comply. He bent over, tying her hands together.

"You can let me go," she said. "I've helped Ben. Doctored her and fed her. I just want to go back to the wagons."

"I wasn't trying to take you," he muttered. He jerked the rope and it cut into her hands. "I don't want to kill you. I just wanted my little girl back."

Felicity had been in the way? That's why he'd lifted her out of the wagon seat. It had happened so fast that she hadn't registered him trying to take Ben. The girl had been frightened by the shooting and holding tightly to Felicity at the time.

"I've got to get back before they realize I'm gone," he muttered. "I wasn't supposed to take her, but I need my little girl."

He sounded mad, as if he was out of touch with reality. He tied off the knot with one more violent tug, Felicity held back a cry as her arms jerked behind her. Her ribs protested the way her shoulders were pulled back. Tears leaked from her eyes.

"Pa, I wanna go back to our wagon," Ben whined.

Their wagon? What did that mean?

He squatted in front of her, putting away his gun in its holster at his belt. He hugged her, then set her back, his hands at her arms while he looked at her.

"We don't have a wagon anymore," he said. "I didn't want to be killed, didn't want them to find you, so I joined up with—with some men. I'm gonna help—help them. And then when we're finished, I'm gonna come back and get you."

"No, Pa! I wanna stay with you," she wailed.

She tried to throw herself at him, but he stood up and gently pushed her away before going to his horse and mounting up. "Stay back," he warned as the horse danced from her wailing.

"Pa! Pa, don't leave!"

But he rode off, over the lip of the small gully he'd sequestered them in and out of sight. Which meant they would be out of sight of the wagon train as well. She could hear far-off shots firing.

"Ben!" Felicity called when the girl raced after him. She only got as far as the top of the gully, slowed by her cast. She flopped down on the ground, sobbing like her life was ending.

Felicity struggled to loosen the bonds at her wrists even as she tried to piece together what had just been revealed.

I didn't want to be killed. Ben's father must have been traveling with that wagon train that had been attacked. But he'd joined up with the gang of thieves who had murdered his friends? It made an awful kind of sense. Felicity knew that human instinct was to survive.

And now he'd chosen to attack Hollis's wagon train. But it was bigger and there were enough men to protect it—she didn't see a way for it to end without death. Maybe death on both sides.

"Ben!" she called. "I need you to untie me."

"I want Pa!" Ben wailed.

Felicity tried to feel the ground behind her with fingers that were slowly going numb. She needed something sharp that might cut through the ropes.

It was all up to her. She'd known for the longest time that she could only rely on herself. That no one else would choose her. Hadn't that been true only minutes ago, when August had been forced to choose between saving her or saving Rachel?

She twisted her wrists, crying out when the movement pulled her ribs and pain sliced through her.

Of course, August had chosen Rachel. She was beautiful and intelligent and in need of a husband. She rubbed some folks on the wagon train the wrong way, but she'd also been displaced, her husband killed, and she was at the end of a pregnancy. With some security and the love of a good man, like August, surely everyone would love her.

It was Felicity left out in the cold. Not chosen.

Just like Celia hadn't wanted her. Just like Father had never stood up for her, never given her the attention she craved, either.

Felicity bowed her head and wept. She didn't want to die out here, didn't want Ben's father to come back and kill her. She wanted to live.

She wanted to be loved.

She wanted August to love her. To choose her.

"I want Pa!" Ben wailed again.

She raised her head, mouth open to snap at the girl. She needed to see sense. But Ben was staring into space, completely forlorn, tears streaking down her face.

She'd said the same words all along. Felicity had thought she was foolish, had tried to tell her that surely her father was dead. But Ben had known, somehow. She'd wanted her father to come back.

And he had.

The little girl had never been shy about demanding what she wanted, even when it had seemed impossible.

She demands what she wants.

Felicity had never done that. Or maybe she had when she'd been small. She'd attempted to climb into her stepmother's lap for a cuddle, once. She couldn't remember if she'd used words. And she'd been rebuffed.

But she'd never asked her father to intervene when Celia had loaded her down with chores. She hadn't stood up for herself when they'd used her egg money to buy that dress for Norah, or when her boss at the dressmaker's had passed over her for the promotion she'd wanted.

She'd been overlooked, hurt, but she hadn't actually asked for what she wanted.

And she hadn't told August how she felt about him.

She'd listened to him tell her about his childhood. She'd felt compassion for the young boy who'd made such a terrible choice. She'd loved him so much she hadn't wanted to ask him to make another choice like that—to choose her. But was she being fair to him—to both of them—by not admitting her feelings?

She owed it to him to tell him the truth. Even if he couldn't choose her.

She renewed her attempts to get out of the ropes as Ben's crying wound down.

"Honey, it's going to be all right," she said in the most soothing voice she could muster.

It might not be. There was still shooting happening. What if August was injured or killed? What about the rest of the wagon train?

She had to escape. Then she recognized a tiny amount of slack in the ropes. Somehow she'd twisted her wrists in just the right way. She held her breath as she worked to slip one hand out of the loops that bound it. When it was finally free, she used nerveless fingers to strip the rope off her other hand.

She shook out her hands, sitting forward to relieve the ache in her ribs. Ben crawled to her, and Felicity pulled the girl into her arms.

They couldn't stay here. She didn't know if Ben's father would come back with a loaded gun. And the wagon train needed help. But she was unarmed, and Ben could barely walk with that cast on.

What now?

Chapter Nineteen

This has to work.

August prayed the words as he mounted up on his horse, just inside the ring of wagons.

Coop had crawled out from under the wagon and now stood only feet away. He pointed to the southwest. "I saw the blue roan take off that direction."

Surprise flashed. August hadn't known the other man had seen, but he was grateful for the information, and grateful for Coop's help.

They were running out of time. It had been almost a half hour since Felicity had been taken—too long.

Rapid-fire gunshots echoed from the eastern side of the wagon train. There were still three riders on this side, but it seemed the bulk of the attack was coming from East of their circle of wagons. August didn't care about the rhyme or reason of it; the fact that there were less bad guys blocking him from getting to Felicity was a good thing.

He nodded to Coop, who tugged his hat down over

his eyes and lifted his rifle in his right hand. In his left was a small wooden keg of gunpowder.

Coop ran out from between the two wagons. At the same time, August raced his horse out of the circle.

The three men that had been riding back and forth reacted almost immediately, the two farthest away turning their horses.

A shot went over August's head.

Coop gave a huge heave and hurled the gunpowder keg as far as he could. It soared through the air and then bounced along the ground.

Wait.

Closer.

August fired when the keg was within twenty feet of the bandits. One shouted and tried to wheel his horse as August's bullet pierced the wood.

The gunpowder exploded with an earsplitting roar and a flash of fire.

Shouts and screams rose from the wagon train, but August ignored everything behind him.

Two of the horses ahead of him reared. Unfortunately, their riders stayed on.

Coop had rolled to the ground after he'd thrown the keg. Now he fired his rifle to give August cover. The man nearest jerked backward and then tumbled off his horse. He didn't get up.

August had taken his shot at the gunpowder quickly, then he'd holstered his rifle and drawn his revolver.

On his horse and with the men reeling from the explosion, he drew close enough to fire at the man in the long black duster. He, too, fell from his horse.

The third man on a tan horse galloped away.

The man August had shot started to get up.

Instead of running back to the wagons, Coop ran toward the men. Now he waved August off, shouting, "Go on, then!"

Coop would take care of the man still struggling to stand, so August didn't waste any more time. He urged his horse into a full out gallop in the direction Coop had pointed moments ago. His heart was pounding, adrenaline pumping through him, sharpening his focus. He didn't know what he would find when he crossed the prairie.

One man had taken Felicity and Ben. But where had he taken them? Had he had help waiting?

August could be riding into a hail of bullets.

He scanned the grass, almost impossible at a full gallop, hoping to see a hoofprint or some sign that he was heading in the right direction.

From a break where the prairie rolled away, August caught sight of a lone rider. He was easily a hundred yards to August's left side and riding in the opposite direction. Toward the wagon train.

August recognized the horse. It was the same man who'd taken the two females.

He might not have even seen August yet. And August couldn't tell exactly where the man had ridden up from. The landscape fell away behind him, so maybe a hidden valley?

But as August guided his horse to head in the direction the man had come from, the man turned his mount too.

August drew his revolver again, though he didn't fire. This man knew where Felicity and Ben were. August wanted him alive.

But the man fired at August, a near miss that kicked up grass near the horse's hooves.

August couldn't risk getting himself killed. Felicity needed him. He prayed she was alive to need him still.

He took aim and fired back.

Blood sprayed. The man stayed on his horse, but the horse balked and then slowed, finally stopping as August approached, warily keeping his gun drawn on the other man.

But the man had dropped his gun. His face was deathly pale. August hopped off his horse, and the man slowly fell to the side and to the ground.

August ran around the horse and knelt beside the man. "Where are they?" he demanded.

He hadn't wanted this. Hated that he'd caused this man such harm. But he'd had no choice.

Only a gurgle escaped the man's lips before he took one shuddering breath and the life faded out of him.

August stood, one hand rested on top of his hat. What now?

He gathered the reins of the man's horse, then rushed back to his own. He took off in the direction the man had come from, riding one horse, leading the other.

"Felicity!" he yelled.

God, please let her answer.

"Ben!"

Nothing.

His heart was hammering for another reason now. Was Felicity already gone? He didn't know if he could survive losing her. He should have told Owen from the beginning how he felt. Maybe this could have been prevented—

He saw hoofprints going off the edge of a gully, dirt that had been disturbed.

When he carefully edged his horse over there, he saw what appeared to be some rope coiled under a tree and grass pressed down like someone had been sitting or struggling there.

No Felicity.

No Ben.

But someone had been here.

Where—?

He guided his horse back up the slope. Surely if she'd gotten loose, Felicity wouldn't have gone down into the gully.

He rode along the gully's edge. Still nothing.

He turned around.

This direction took him closer to the river, farther from the caravan. Would Felicity have come this way?

Was this a lost cause?

His mind was whirling, and it took him a moment to register what he saw.

The buffalo herd, or at least a part of it. On this side of the river.

And a woman and little girl standing far too close to them, waving their arms and shouting.

She was alive! Joy and relief swirled through him at the same time as stark fear struck.

What were they doing? They could be killed if one of those animals charged.

He pushed his horse to a run, forcing the other to follow. Several of the animals scattered as he neared.

Felicity saw him. He saw her turn, saw the recognition cross her expression. She grabbed Ben's arm and pointed.

He was close enough to dismount at a run, trusting his horse to stick around.

She rushed toward him, half-lifting and half-dragging poor Ben with her broken leg.

He reached for Felicity first, cupping her face in his hands, glancing down her body, looking for injury. Scratches covered her arms and a bead of blood leaked from one on her cheek. There were tears in her eyes, and he couldn't resist any longer, not when she looked hale and healthy. He took her carefully in his arms, just in case there was an injury he couldn't see, and he pulled Ben into the embrace at his side.

Felicity burrowed her face into his shoulder, a little sob escaping.

"I thought you were hurt or... worse." He swallowed hard.

She gasped a little when his jaw brushed her temple. He leaned back a bit, brushing away the hair at her temple, where an ugly bump bloomed with a purple and green bruise.

He clenched his teeth. "You *are* hurt."

Tears spilled over. "I'm all right. We're all right."

She was so beautiful, so full of life as she tried to brush away her tears. He kept his hand on Ben's shoulder but wound his arm around Felicity's waist and bent his head to kiss her.

She met his seeking lips and returned his kiss with a fervor that told him her relief matched his. She tasted of tears and hope and home. He never wanted to let her go again.

But Ben was tugging on his arm. He reluctantly broke the kiss.

"What're you doing with my pa's horse?"

* * *

Felicity watched the confusion and then realization cross August's expression—along with something else. Something like . . . guilt.

"I found him." His voice was a little bit broken. When she sent him a questioning glance, he shook his head slightly.

And then she knew.

Ben's pa was gone.

With conflicting emotions, she put her arm around Ben's shoulders. "We still have work to do."

"What're you doing with those buffalo?" The tender affection in his voice made her desperately want to be back in his arms, to tell him everything that was in her heart.

But now wasn't the time.

She could still hear faint gunshots. They seemed more rapid now. Had the bandits grown desperate?

"Once I got free of where he'd tied me up, I knew we couldn't just run back to the wagons. And I'm unarmed. I thought maybe we could give the bandits a taste of their own medicine if I could frighten the buffalo into running that way."

As she'd been taken, she'd seen that the wagons were almost circled up. Surely the travelers would be safe; the buffalo would likely divert around them. It would be the bandits who might get trampled.

August looked at her with an incredulous expression —and then he swept her into his arms, peppering her cheeks with kisses. "You're a genius."

Heat blazed in her cheeks, but she couldn't stop beaming up at him.

His eyes shadowed with concern. "Can you ride?"

She nodded. She'd been jerked around and tweaked her ribs in the struggle, but if it meant rescuing Abigail and Evangeline and everyone else, she could bear the pain.

He boosted her into the saddle of his horse, giving her knee a quick squeeze before he picked up Ben and climbed into the saddle of the other horse.

"Put a bit of distance between you and the buffalo," he said. "If they charge, they're extremely dangerous."

He told her which direction to ride, and they spread out behind the nearest animals.

He raised his revolver and set off three rapid shots. She shouted and waved her skirt. To his credit, August's horse stood steady while the nearest buffalo shied away.

"Get on!" she shouted at the top of her lungs. Her voice box ached.

But when August fired another shot, two of the animals took off.

And more followed, until the entire herd began moving toward the wagon train.

"It's working!" she cried.

August still wore a mask of concern, holding Ben with one hand in front of him in the saddle. He nodded for her to follow behind the herd, keeping her distance.

Where they might have veered off, he rode up behind them and waved his hat and shouted. They re-routed straight toward the circled wagons, now in sight.

From her slightly elevated position, Felicity saw one man's horse get swept into the mass of moving brown bodies. She held her breath, remembering the tenor of their hooves, big and heavy. How they'd almost knocked down the wagon.

But the herd split almost exactly in two and rounded the circled wagons on both sides, leaving them unscathed. She and August rode behind at a slower pace. As they neared camp, they were met with cheers and shouts.

Leo and Hollis were already on horseback and ordering men to mount up.

"We'll corner whoever's left," Hollis shouted.

But August was already off his horse, Ben on the ground beside him, reaching up to help Felicity down. Once her feet were on the ground, he doffed his hat to someone.

Coop.

What was that about?

There was no time to figure it out because Owen stormed over. He had a white bandage wrapped around his upper left arm, over his shirt.

"What were you thinking?" he demanded.

August answered without looking away from her eyes. "I did what I had to do."

"Let's join the others," Owen said irritably.

And now August did glance at his brother. He shook his head slowly as his hand came to rest on Felicity's waist. "I'm not going."

Owen looked as if he wanted to slug his brother. A muscle ticked in his jaw. "The camp needs you."

August was completely calm as he looked around. "Camp is here. And people inside this circle need help, too."

Felicity hadn't taken time to look around in the excitement of getting back into camp. But she now saw Rachel sitting on the ground next to a body.

Oh no.

Rachel was dry-eyed and silent, staring off into the distance at nothing.

Abigail and Alice and Evangeline were moving from wagon to wagon, each at different places in the circle, checking on folks. There were at least two men sitting on the ground, looking dazed. One held a cloth on an obvious wound to his shoulder.

Owen's stare moved to August's hand on Felicity's back. She might've flinched under the intensity of Owen's gaze if August hadn't leaned in even closer to her. He was like a wall of comfort.

Owen didn't say anything else, only frowned fiercely and walked away.

Ben had scrambled into the wagon bed. "Kitty! Kitty!"

August brushed a kiss on Felicity's forehead. "Will you be all right if I check on Frank Teller?"

She glanced at the man sitting near his wagon, blood seeping through his fingers as they covered a wound on his leg.

"I'm fine. I'll see if Alice has some bandages and water."

He sent her a grateful look.

It was natural to slip back into the role of helper. She moved around camp fetching and carrying supplies when they weren't too heavy, offering comfort to women or children deeply shaken by the events of the day.

But there was something different about working like this, while August did the same across camp. Every time she looked up, she caught him watching her. He offered a tender smile or winked at her. And his attention made all the difference.

She wasn't alone anymore.

August had come for her.

By the time the sun had risen overhead, she'd lost sight of him, and her ribs were protesting every little movement. She knew she needed to sit down and rest, so she headed back to her wagon to find a patch of shade and check on Ben.

She almost walked past August. He was crouched on the ground near Rachel, who hadn't moved all morning. She must be in shock. From what Felicity understood, she'd witnessed Daniel's death.

"I'll help you in any way I can," August said quietly. "But I can't marry you." He looked up and their gazes collided. "Not when my heart belongs to someone else."

Felicity's own heart began to pound. This wasn't a moment to interrupt. She kept walking, hiding herself in the shade behind her wagon, leaning one shoulder against the conveyance. She pressed her hand to her chest.

Had August meant what he'd said?

A few moments later she felt him draw near. She turned to face him. He looked both serious and gentle.

"I should've said something before," she blurted.

"About my heart. That it belongs to you. I was. . .I was scared to admit it." She'd been frightened to ask him to choose her.

He stepped close and tucked a piece of hair behind her ear. "I was scared, too. Of making a mistake. But my heart's been true this entire time. It hasn't wavered. And I don't think that falling for you was a mistake."

His words soaked into her heart like water filling in dusty cracks after a terrible drought.

Tears pricked her eyes, but she refused to let them fall when it meant blurring the loving look in his eyes.

"I love you, Felicity."

She couldn't argue with the intensity and gentleness of his voice. One tear slipped down her cheek. She laughed as she brushed it away. "I love you, too."

He leaned down and pressed a gentle kiss to her lips. She fell into his embrace and kissed him back. Kissing him felt like all the dreams she had never dared to dream. It felt like home.

The sound of shouting and clapping interrupted them. But the celebration wasn't directed at them, though Felicity was blushing as if it had been.

Through a parting in the wagon circle, Hollis and the other men rode in, with several horses being led by their reins. Lying across the backs of each was one of the bandits.

The travelers crowded around Hollis on his horse. She joined August, clasping her hand in his. They hung back at the back of the crowd.

"Several of 'em got trampled. Two we took out. They won't be bothering us or anyone else anymore."

Someone shouted, "Why'd they attack?"

"Wanted to steal our stock and supplies, I'd wager," said Hollis.

The group broke up, and Hollis made his way toward August. "We've got you to thank. We'd still have been trapped in the circle if it wasn't for those buffalo."

August shook his head. "Wasn't my idea. It was Felicity's."

Hollis's frank gaze took her in. "Then I guess I'll say thanks to you."

A blush filled her cheeks.

August squeezed her hand. "She's amazing. We're lucky to have her on the wagon train."

She basked in his admiration. She didn't know what the future held, but with August standing beside her, she had only peace.

Chapter Twenty

"Morning."

Felicity turned at the voice—August's voice. It was early, the sky still dark and scattered with sleepy stars. Silver lined the horizon.

After two long days of constant travel, totaling over forty miles, Hollis had called for a late start this morning, a chance for everyone to catch their breath. But Felicity had woken early and crept out of the tent and over to the closest fire.

And August had found her there.

"Morning." She returned his greeting with a smile.

He came close to brush a kiss on her hair. He had a cup of coffee in hand and the sharp scent permeated the air. He offered the cup to her. She took a drink, warmed by the intimacy of sharing it.

She leaned her shoulder into his side and his arm came easily around her as he settled her beside him, sharing his warmth in the early morning coolness.

"How're the ribs?" he asked quietly.

"Better. A little," she qualified when he tilted his head to look at her.

The first morning after the attack when she and Ben had been separated from the wagon, she'd woken so stiff and sore that she could barely move. She'd been confined to the wagon most of that first day. Yesterday she'd had more mobility.

Abigail emerged from the tent. She had the kitten in her arms and her nose crinkled up in disgust. "This ornery thing."

Felicity barely stifled a smile. "Morning."

Ben had finally given the kitten a name. Whiskers. Felicity and the kitten had made their peace only after Felicity had found him cowering in a neighbor's wagon after the dust up. Felicity had wooed Whiskers out of his hiding place with a piece of boiled chicken and he'd spent the evening following every step she took. Though the kitten could still surprise her with unexpected attacks, she and Whiskers had started what would possibly become a lifelong friendship.

August squeezed her shoulders gently. "I thought I might scout on foot this morning. You want to come with me?"

Her heart warmed. He'd sought her out to ask her to go along with him? Of course, she wanted to go.

"I'll keep an eye on Ben, if she wakes," Abigail offered.

A few more folks began stirring around camp as August stopped momentarily to put away the now-empty coffee cup and pick up his rifle. And then they slipped between two wagons and out into the wide prairie beyond.

August didn't hesitate to clasp her hand in his.

"I've never been scouting before," she murmured. "What should we be looking for?"

He held his rifle at his side, pointed at the ground. She knew now that he was the kind of man who always wanted to be prepared.

"Anything that might be a danger to the caravan," August said. "Animals, something in the landscape."

He didn't mention the human danger they'd already faced. The men from camp had held a long meeting on the evening of the attack, discussing what they knew and trying to figure out why the gang of thieves had attacked and killed one wagon train and then theirs.

August had been quiet and serious when he'd come to her after the meeting. There weren't many answers. The men might've been from a wagon train that passed through last year and didn't make it to Oregon. Or men who'd moved West from the cities and decided that survival was too difficult, that killing and stealing was easier.

They were gone now, and Hollis would report what had happened to the fort they'd reach in another ten days. No one knew what had happened to the stolen oxen and supplies from Rachel's wagon train. Hollis was determined to deliver information to the soldiers at the fort. Maybe they would track down the missing beasts.

It was frightening to think of traveling for the rest of the summer and into the fall. What if there were other men out there who wanted to harm them?

But she had some comfort. After Felicity and August had run the buffalo, Hollis had brought the saddled horses, now riderless, to her. He'd thanked her again for her help and gifted the horses to her.

Out here, a horse was a valuable commodity. It wasn't food that would carry them to the Willamette Valley, but she could trade the horses, if need be. There were nine of them, and nine saddles. They had recovered the horse that Daniel had let loose.

Felicity wasn't penniless anymore.

And in the end, Abigail had been correct. God had provided. Not only the horses, but His protection for Felicity, August, Ben, the entire wagon train. She would never forget His presence when she'd been tied up beneath that plum shrub.

The sky had lightened around them as they walked, softening into shades of pale pink and faint orange. She was slightly out of breath by the time they hiked up a rocky promontory that looked over the area around them. August drew her up beside him and motioned her to stop. She stood at his side, soaking in the view.

"No more buffalo?" she asked.

"No more buffalo."

From this vantage point, it was easy to see the change in the landscape. Where the prairie had stretched mostly flat with some undulations behind them, ahead was a more sandy, rocky soil. Vegetation was sparser, and she could see the outline of rolling hills in the far distance. It was beautiful, wild country.

"How's Ben?" August asked as he scanned the land in all directions.

"It's been a difficult couple of days."

Riders had gone out to collect all the bodies of the outlaws. Some of the camp had argued that violent men like them didn't deserve a decent burial, but ultimately Hollis had the final say.

Ben had been present when someone had laid out her father's body with the others. She'd wailed and sobbed, hugging his leg. She'd been nigh inconsolable since.

"My bullet killed him," August said.

"I know," she returned softly.

Over the past two days, Hollis had pushed the group to travel so many miles, and they'd worked so hard, that she hadn't had time for more than a basic conversation with August, checking in before they separated to their own tents for the night. He hadn't told her outright, until now, but she'd seen it in his face that morning of the attack.

Now she read the pain in the fine lines around his eyes. His gaze was far off, his mind obviously in the past.

"I was going to ride around—avoid him. He came at me, shot at me—" His voice broke slightly.

She moved closer, slipping into the space next to his side, putting her arms around his waist. His arm came naturally around her shoulder.

"You were defending yourself," she said. "If he'd hit you—" Now it was her turn to catch her breath, the thought of August being the one who'd been killed cutting deeply inside her. She couldn't stand the thought.

"You think she'll ever forgive me?"

"She doesn't need to know, not right now. When she's older, when she can understand better. . ." Felicity wished she could give him a firm answer. She was still struggling to come to terms with what she'd learned about Ben's father in those frantic few minutes. He'd loved his daughter, that much was obvious. But he'd made some bad choices. And those choices had consequences.

"I'm going to keep her with me," Felicity said. "I'm not old enough to take the place of her mother, but I love her. She'll need someone to look after her."

When he glanced down at her, she saw the softness in his eyes. "You've a good heart."

It wasn't the first time he'd said it, but his words still made warmth bloom in her chest.

There were several beats of silence between them, then he spoke with his gaze focused outward. "Owen and I have a homestead, back in California. It's a real pretty place at the base of a mountain. Good hunting. Some land for farming. I was born there. Ma and Pa are buried there."

"And you'll go back."

He nodded. "Probably winter in Oregon first." He sighed. "Owen owns the land by birthright. I don't know. . . maybe he'll sell it to me."

She wasn't supposed to know about the marriage wager. Was August admitting that he was going to lose it? Or was this about the fraught silences she'd noticed between the two brothers these past days?

He moved away and turned to face her. The sun was up over the horizon now. It gilded the tips of his hair and eyelashes in gold. She took in the seriousness of his expression and her stomach dipped.

"There's nothing I want more than for you to come to California with me." He swallowed hard, a show of emotion that she knew he shared only with her. "As my wife."

Her stomach dipped again, like she was standing at the edge of a precipice and looking down. A feeling both terrifying and exhilarating.

He wasn't finished. "Felicity, you bring such a gentle joy to my life. The way you care for the people around you, and the way you light up the night sky just by being under it. I love you. Please, will you marry me?"

She couldn't help the happy tears blurring her vision. "Yes. Oh, August, I love you, too."

He swept her into his arms, sharing a deep kiss with her that felt as if it sealed everything they'd just agreed on.

She would be his wife. He would be her husband.

He loved her, cherished her. It was there in his words.

He'd chosen her above all else.

His love soothed the wounds of her past, gave her hope and security for the future. Whatever came, they would face it together.

"I don't want to wait," he said, when they broke apart, breathing heavily. "Hollis said he'd marry us this morning, if you were agreeable. I want to be a family with you."

She beamed at him. "I want that too. Yes, I'll marry you this morning."

He brushed one more kiss on her cheek. "We'd better go then. I've got to break the news to my brother."

She wished she could ease the tension in his voice, but she had to settle for clasping his hand in hers as they walked back to the wagon train.

* * *

August splashed cold water over his face and head. It trickled down his back, sending a shiver down his spine.

The creek was quiet during this morning time. Many of the women from camp had spent the early hours washing clothes and dishes, something they hadn't had time for the past two days of tireless travel.

But now it was only him and the soft coo of a dove somewhere overhead in the scrub oak trees. He'd left Felicity at her wagon, where Abigail had squealed over the news of their impending wedding and promptly shooed him away so Felicity could have some time to get ready.

He was ready. This was the right decision. He felt it, deep in his bones.

He stared down at his reflection in the trickling water, hardly able to believe the blessings God had poured down in his life. Felicity had agreed to marry him. They would make their life together. Maybe on the family homestead. Maybe somewhere else. That would depend on Owen.

They'd start out as a ready-made family, with Ben a part of their lives together. The girl had been through hard times, but she was resilient, intelligent, and sweet. Felicity seemed to think she'd be all right.

He glanced up at the crack of a twig under a boot.

"This a private bath time?" Coop stood several yards down the stream, a shaving straight razor in hand.

"No. Not private."

Coop sat down on the water's edge, taking off his boots and unrolling his socks before he plunked his feet in the water, wetting the hem of his pants. His movements were sluggish and jerky. His eyes were bloodshot, like he hadn't slept all night. Or like he'd drunk himself to sleep in the wee hours.

August knew Leo and Alice worried about their brother. Coop had demons of his own, ones that August didn't know a thing about. It was more than obvious that they'd chased him down last night.

"I haven't had a chance to thank you," August said, standing straight. "I don't know what would've happened to Felicity and Ben if you hadn't helped me with that distraction."

Coop spread a lather of soap on his neck and chin. "Aw, shucks. Make me blush."

Maybe he didn't want the praise, but August felt the need to say it. "I love her, and you helped me get out there to rescue her. Thank you for what you did."

Coop ran the razor over his jaw with a *snick*. "Maybe you tell Leo all that and he'll get off my case. He was spitting fire that I wasted his precious gunpowder."

There was a bitterness in Coop's voice, a tension between the brothers that August had seen time and again. He owed Coop a favor. "I'll replace it."

Coop shaved another strip in silence. Then another. Finally, his lips twisted as he wiped the blade on his pants leg. "Don't bother. He'll only find something else to grumble about."

Then August still owed the man a debt. "You ever need anything, you come to me."

Coop half-smiled. August didn't know whether the other man had taken him serious at all, but he'd tried.

He headed back to camp, his thoughts on tracking down his brother to talk.

Turned out he didn't have to look. Owen was waiting

for him on the outside of the circle of wagons, arms crossed.

August steeled himself. His brother had barely spoken to him since he'd ignored the commands Owen had given in the wake of the attack.

Owen had kept busy in meetings with Hollis, comforting and helping the other passengers in his role as captain, while August had managed his wagon and helped with Felicity's wagon, and scouted their route in the mornings and during the time they traveled. They'd been assigned different watches.

But it sure seemed Owen was ready to face off and have this out now.

August went in swinging. "I'm sorry I can't marry Rachel."

Owen's eyes narrowed. He glanced to the side, shifting very slightly on one foot. Rachel seemed to continue to be a sore subject for him.

August took a deep breath. he wanted to smooth things over with his brother. "I know you wanted me to marry her—"

"I want you to be happy," Owen grumbled.

August drew up short, his brother's words not making a lick of sense. "What?"

"I want you to be happy," Owen said. He didn't crack a smile. "If Felicity makes you happy, you should be with her."

"She does." The words were out before he'd even had time to think them. They were true. He loved Felicity fiercely and deeply and couldn't imagine his life without her in it.

Owen nodded. "Then it's the right decision." He

inhaled deeply, nostrils flaring. "And. . . I'm going to try and step back and not interfere so much in your life."

August hadn't expected that.

Owen wasn't done. "Since we were kids, you always looked at me like I could do no wrong. I guess it went to my head. Or became a habit. I'll always want to protect my baby brother."

August warmed inside at his brother's words.

"But you're a grown man now. One with a good many skills and a good head on your shoulders. You don't need me to make your decisions for you."

August shook his head. "No. But I may need your advice. What do I know about being a husband or a papa?"

Now Owen shook his head. "I don't know those things either."

"You know about being a strong leader. A man of God. That's what matters."

Owen moved forward and clapped a hand on August's shoulder. "So do you."

Nothing could heal the deep sadness August felt when he thought about Ma and what she'd suffered, his part in her death. But these moments together healed a rift with his brother, one that had been a wound for a long time.

"You'd better go find Hollis. I think your bride is waiting for you."

August didn't walk off immediately. He stepped closer and pulled his brother into a hug. Owen came a mite grudgingly, groaning when August accidentally brushed against the bullet wound in his arm. They didn't often show affection this way. But he slapped

August's back and August didn't bother trying to hide the tears he wiped away. He would always need his brother.

"Stand up with me," he said.

Owen nodded.

They met Hollis in the center of the ring of wagons. Most people were packed and ready to head out, happy to celebrate this moment with two of their own. Felicity had become something of a celebrity among the travelers as everyone knew she'd been the one to save them from the attackers.

She was beautiful as she joined them, her hair pulled back at her nape. She wore a pale blue dress that he'd seen before. She looked so beautiful she took his breath away, and he told her so.

She blushed prettily.

They joined hands and stood in front of Hollis. Abigail stood at Felicity's side, with Ben pale and quiet behind her. Owen stood just behind August. The moment felt solemn and weighty as Hollis explained that they were making vows before God, joining their lives together.

His emotional Felicity got teary-eyed when she repeated her vows, and he found himself misty when he said his, too. And when Hollis announced August could kiss his bride, a whoop went up from the assembled crowd.

He kissed her tenderly, there under the wide blue sky with their friends looking on. It only made the moment more meaningful that Owen stood beside him, their relationship stronger than ever. He couldn't know what would happen in the future, but he would rely on the God who blessed him so richly to protect his new family.

And he'd be thankful for his blessings every day.

* * *

Not long after the wedding, Owen approached the creek, picking his way through the woods so he wouldn't disturb her. The place where he'd been winged by a bullet pulsed with a dull, never-ending ache. Rachel knelt on the bank of the little tributary, her hands submerged in the water, suds trailing downstream. She scrubbed her hands together, and he realized she was washing out her dress.

She owned exactly two dresses. One she wore now, that Felicity had modified to fit her in this late stage of her pregnancy. And the one she was washing, the dress she'd been wearing when she'd been found in the woods.

He didn't want to know so much about her. How many dresses she owned. That she was restless at night and didn't sleep much. How she looked when she grieved.

No one else seemed to be aware that she was down here. The rest of camp was packed up. Folks were standing around, congratulating August and Felicity on their nuptials. It was only a matter of minutes before Hollis would blow the bugle.

But Rachel seemed to be in no hurry.

He stood where he was, several yards downstream and half-hidden behind a tree. She'd been nothing but trouble since his brother had found her out in the woods.

Trouble for Owen.

Who couldn't stop thinking about her. Especially since he'd watched Daniel's life leaking out between his hands.

He hadn't put Daniel on that wagon or forced him to take off from the main caravan. He'd been shouting for the other man to stop and take cover when the outlaws had started shooting. Owen had shot back, wanting to scare them off.

In the melee, he couldn't be sure whose bullet had hit Daniel, his or one of the outlaws'.

It shouldn't matter. Daniel was gone. Maybe that was for the better. The man had been cruel, drowned his grief in a bottle, said things to his sister that no man should ever say to a woman. Struck her, even.

As far as Owen was concerned, good riddance.

But since Owen had delivered Daniel's body into the circle of wagons, Rachel had shut down.

Gone was the woman who had harangued every family on the wagon train, trying to find a horse or some transportation to take her back East.

Gone was the woman who'd helped every woman who would let her, toted wash water, made supper, watched children.

It was as if Rachel had died too, and only her shadow remained. She was meek and quiet, barely ate. He saw her staring blankly into a fire when he woke and last thing before bed.

He wasn't supposed to feel guilt over her situation.

But he did.

And it made him itchy.

And that made him mad.

He made his way up the creek bank, making no effort to hide or quiet his approach.

She didn't look up.

His temper rumbled like a sleeping dragon, a wisp of smoke on an exhale. Why couldn't the woman do anything the way he might expect?

He cleared his throat.

When she still didn't look up, he asked, "You doin' all right?"

She didn't answer him, just kept scrubbing that dress under the water. He'd been close enough to see the fraying hems and an elbow that had already been patched. If she wasn't careful, she'd scrub the thing to threads.

Silence reigned for a moment that lengthened into awkwardness and that dragon that was his temper flared its nostrils, a lick of flame escaping. "I asked you a question."

She looked up at him, and he saw only dullness in her eyes. "I'm fine. Is that what you want to hear?"

If her words had held any of the old fire she always seemed to flame at him, he would've kept his trap shut. But she spoke almost in monotone.

"Is the baby all right? After that fall?" He'd been too far away, on horseback, to do anything when her scoundrel of a brother had shoved her off the wagon. He'd seen it, though, and something inside of him had raged when she'd hit the ground with a limp thud.

She shrugged. Her indifference woke up the dragon.

"I'm trying to help," he snapped. "The least you could do is answer me."

Something inside her seemed to snap, too. She threw

down the dress in the water, splashing droplets everywhere. "The least I can do?" She struggled to her feet, her eyes now flashing fire. "I don't want your help. Your help got my brother killed."

Her words hit him like a slug to the stomach, stealing his air. He had done that. It didn't matter if her brother was a scoundrel. Owen had been responsible.

"You're still stuck with me until we reach the fort." This time, his words held only a little of the bite from earlier.

Tears sprang to her eyes before she turned her head and stomped after the dress that had quickly floated downstream—in his direction.

He took two steps into the water and caught it, his wound pulsing with the effort. He held the sopping mass over the creek as water ran down in rivulets.

She didn't want to be left at the fort. That much was obvious. He didn't blame her. The fort would be filled with crass men, and who knew how long it might be before someone was willing to take her on—maybe an eternity if she still intended to go back East.

She firmed her lips and her chin tipped up. His stomach dipped at the show of attitude. She might be grieving, but she was still herself. That attitude was just hiding under the layers of pain.

She reached for the dress.

He took the time to squeeze most of the water out of it before he handed it to her.

She didn't say thank you.

He shook his head. What had he expected? "Hollis will call for us to move out in a few minutes."

He was done here. He'd told her what he needed to say.

"If you really wanted to help, you'd find me a way back East," she muttered to the ground.

He stopped from where he'd moved a step away. Put his hands on his hips as he faced her again.

"Everyone here is traveling West," he reminded her as gently as he could.

Maybe not so gentle, judging by the stubborn twist of her lips.

"What you need is a husband." The words were out before he realized he was going to say them.

Fire flashed in her eyes. "You offering?"

No.

The answer rang inside him like a bell, clear and loud. He wasn't husband material, and she sure as shootin' wasn't a match for him.

But there was a part of him that niggled like a tooth waiting to fall out. He had been responsible, at least in part, for Daniel's death.

Did that make him responsible for her?

"I guess I am."

She looked as surprised as he felt that he'd said the words.

But she didn't give him a chance to change his mind. "Fine."

Fine.

Only it wasn't fine at all.

What had he done?

* * *

Thank you for reading A TRAIL UNTAMED. I hope you loved August and Felicity's romance. You'll see them again in WILD HEART'S HAVEN...

Rachel never wanted to travel into the wilderness. The westward trail has stolen everything from her. Her home. Her family. Her husband. Now a match made out of necessity has trapped her in a marriage with a man she can't stand.

Owen likes Rachel about as much as his horse likes a burr under its saddle. She's bossy and stubborn with an independent streak a mile wide. And a baby on the way.

He can't help feeling responsible for the prickly mother-to-be. A marriage of convenience is the right thing to do. But that doesn't mean he has to like it. He just has to survive it until they reach Oregon.

ONE CLICK WILD HEART'S HAVEN NOW >

For my Family.

Acknowledgments

With thanks to my dear friend Benita, who was an early reader of this manuscript.

Gratitude to readers Bonnie and Cindy, who suggested the name for the kitten on this book cover. Also to EC, who suggested Ben's name.

Also thank you to my proofreaders Lillian, Mary-Ellen, Benecia, and Shelley for helping me clean up all the little errors.

A special thank you for my readers

To my readers, both old and new, this book is for you.

Thank you for picking up not just this book, but the ones that came before it. Whether you've been with me from the start or just joined, your support is truly appreciated.

I hope these books provide you with a sense of escape, introduce you to interesting characters, and always leave you pondering the intricacies of love.

With sincere thanks to (listed in alphabetical order by first name:

Adelina, Adriana, Aitijhya Kar, Alice Nieuwendijk, Alice Ruth Fischer, Alice Wiest, Alicia Cullum, Allison D. Proctor, Amanda Lam, Amanda Rollins, Amy Farmer, Amy K Shippy, Amy Smith, Andi P, Angela Smeilus, Angeline Farrow-Douglas, Anita, Anita Rohn, Anita Say Holquist, Ann Badder, Anna May Braley, Annette, Araceli Martinez, Araina, Aubrey Ann DeBaar, Aubrey DeBaar, Barb Beyer, Barb Malone, Barbara A Weintz, Barbara Irene James, Becky Williams, Beth Maddux, Beth Riggen, Bette Lopez, Betty Weaver Smith, Bettye Short, Bevie, Bill Fuller, Bobbie Oliver Turner, Bobbie Sue Brown, Bobo, Bonnie Kaiser, Bonnie MacPherson Allen, Brenda, Brenda Coulter, Brenda Witt, Bridgette K.

Shippy, Bridgette Shippy, Brie Wallace, Brooke, Buckshot, bunnydoodles, Caitlyn Santi, Callie Walters, Carol Angleton Bradford, Carol Bishop, Carole Keaten, Caroline Hattrich, Carolyn Baird, Carolyn Hobbs, Carrie, Catherine McAnda, Catherine Taylor, Cecilia Garrett, Charlie Doodle, Charlotte H. Siepka, Chasity McPeek, Cheryl Hart, Cheryn Porter, Chris Meiser, Christa Skordili, Christiana Dawn Scott, Christie Davis, Christina McCutcheon, Cindy G, Cindy Lou Petty, Cindy Rosinski, Cindy Salazar, Cindy VanHoose, Cindy Woolard, Clara Page, Claudia Jackson, Cloe Caldwell, Colleen Fernandes, Corinne Sorensen, Crystal Stacey, Danyelle Wadsworth, Darla McCarty, Darla Stapleton, Dawn, Dawn Matthews Medlock, Dawne Itnyre, DeAnn Scarborough, Deanna, Deb Hughes, Debbie Hammer, Debbie Hammer, Debbie Kubacki, Debi Gillam, Deborah Brantley, Deborah L. Dumm, Debra A. Fiebig-Kubacki, Debra K Gallagher, Debra Rylander, Dellas Anderton, Denyse, Diana Hardt, Diane Boyd, Diane Lethbridge, Diane Robeck, Donita, Donna Beckham, Donna Bell, Donna Bouchard, Donna Dean, Donna Duke, Donna Marie, Donna Rodgers, Doreen, Dorine, Doris hicks, Edwina Kiernan, EJ Derenzy, Elaine Kiefer, Elaine Mulder, Elaine Shildmyer Oursler, Elsie Weihrauch, Emily Winters, Erin, ErmaEdge, Eva Ruby Fowles Fielding, Evelyn Lord, Fern Peña, Fonda, Fran Breece, Fran Scruggs, Fran Siecko, Freda Frost, Gail E Hollingsworth, Gayle, Genie Baker, Gerry Brown, Ginger Kemp, Ginna Missimer, Glenda Kochany, Glenda Wray Jennings, Harmony Music, Heather Joy Sullivan, HeidiLorin Callies, Holley Harbin, Holly Bleggi, Holly Williamson, Ingemar Jonathon Bjornson, Jacalyn

Callaway Ford, Jane, Jane Marler, Janene Woodard, Janet Demaree, Janet La Grasta, Janice J Grogan, Jasmine McGhee, Jeanne Wright, Jeff Stutsman, Jeminka Van Rieck, Jenn Kolacinski Neitzke, Jennifer C., Jennifer Greer, Jenny-Lynn Fricke, Jessica Baker, Jessica Letourneau, Jill Dailey Knight, Jo, Joan DeLeon, Joan Nolan, JoAnn Copley, Joanne McGee, Jodi Baysden, Jodi Shadden, John Bradley, John Kruijne, Jolie E. Zeller, Joy Anderson, Joy Kendall, Joyce Marie Rehkugler, Judith Ann (Jude), Judy, Judy Boes, Judy Ward, Julia Anne Cooper, Julie A Bryson, Julie E. Finlinson, Julie van Heerden, Julieanne, June Nelson, Kailey Bechtel, Kara Aikala, Karen Sipe, Karen Waymire Zimmerman, Kathryn McQueeny, Kathy and Jenny, Kathy Atkinson, Kathy Danheim, Kay R., Kelly Rhoads, Kerry Bell, Kim Wong, Kimberly Bowie, Kimberly Edgeworth, Kindra, Kris Fontenot, Kristie, Kristie de Wit, Kunita Gear, Kylie Mulvaney, LaKesia Campbell, Launa, Laurie Johnston RN, Leann Kasper, Leiah, Lelian Omega Garces Espinosa, Lettica, Linda Bellar Tucker, Linda D. McFarland, Linda Farabaugh, Linda Gholson Ward, Linda Locklear, Linda Wesson, Lisa Lagnese, Lisa McElveen Ramsing, Lonzine Lee, Lora Musikantow, Lorene Rhiddlehoover, Loretta, LORI IBARRA, Lori Raines, Lorna J Finch aka Jaynie, Lorri J. Harris-Wingo, Louise, Louise, Lynne Alice, Lynne Myers, Mae Matthis Parsons, Mae S. Carr, Mandi Arndt, Marcia Rose, Margaret N, Margie Harris, Margie Rico, Maria Anna Taylor, MariaElena, Marianne, Marianne Hughes, Marianne K., Marilú Wright, Marlene Moore, Mary Ann Speel, Mary G. Johnson, Mary Josephine Carlson, mary k burkett, Mary L. Briere, Mary R Martin, Mary Stalnaker,

Melissa Hartwell, Melody Adina, Michael D Roberts, Michaela, Michele Galloway, Michele Rolfe, Michelle Rhoden, Michelle Spann, Mindy Flow, Mindy M. Bormann, Misty G, MONIQUE COCANOUGHER, Mrs. Daniel (Lynne) Arney Traxler, Mrs. Joy Helmuth, Myra D Hyer, Myrna Hagler, Nancy Ashby, Nancy Scallion-Wood, Natasha P., Natividad Mejia, Nicole House, Nikki S., ODETTE, Ojone, Pamela, Pamela Andrews, Pamela Campbell, Pamela Kyzer, Pat Goplen, Patricia A.Goplen, Patricia Gogick, Patricia Rytter, Patti Pierce, Patti Rytter, Patty Watson, Paula Louise Smith, Paula Magnus, Peggy Sue Burton, Phyllis Bullock, PJL, Polly N. Lico, Priscila Perales, R.A. Herbert, R.C.Carpenter, Rachiel Celenia Soliz, Rhea Piziali, Robin C.Justus, Robin Elizabeth Inabnitt, Robin Kay, Rosemarie, Rosemarie Andreano, Rosemary H, Rowena Louise Pike, Ruth Ann Campbell, Ruthe Threet, Sadra Lee, Sally Childs, Sandi Wynn, Sara Aimeé Herrick, Sara White, Sarah Hume, Shannon Sharp, Shannon wright, Shari, Shari Lane, Sharon L Lee, Sharon Marks, Sharon Meier, Sharon Meier Vince, Sharon W. Steward, Shelley Crews, Shelly Spence, Sherilyn Pickels, Sherry, Sherry Brown, Sherry Kaufmann, Shirley Brooks, Shirley Collins, Shirley Prater, Sonja Jane, Sonja Nishimoto, Sonnie Duchesne, Stephanie Fisher, Stephanie Halcomb, Suzanne Silver, Tami W., Tamlin le Roux, Tammy Lever, Tanis Dixie, Tanya, Taylen M, Teresa Lynn Walden, Teresa M., Teresa Murphy, Teresa West, Teri Ruth, Terre Sexton, Terri McNabb, Terri Miller, Terri St.Clair, Thea Ferreira, Thyra Talento Zeiher, Tina Laws, Tina Richer, Toni F., Tonya Taylor, Tracie Joyner, Treasa George-Price,

Trina Boston, Twila Boaz, Valancy, Valinda Armstrong,
Valynda, Vickie Whaley Bright, Viola Frere-Martin,
Violetta, Virginia Campbell, Vivian Pearson, Willette
Houston, Yvette

Want to connect online? Here's where you can find me:

Get new release alerts

Follow me on Amazon
Follow me on Bookbub
Follow me on Goodreads

Connect on the web

www.lacywilliams.net
lacy@lacywilliams.net

Social media

Also by Lacy Williams

Christmas Bells and Wedding Vows (anthology)

Wagon Train Matches

A Trail So Lonesome

Trail of Secrets

A Trail Untamed

Wild Heart's Haven

Wind River Hearts series (historical romance)

Marrying Miss Marshal

Counterfeit Cowboy

Cowboy Pride

The Homesteader's Sweetheart

Courted by a Cowboy

Roping the Wrangler

Return of the Cowboy Doctor

The Wrangler's Inconvenient Wife

A Cowboy for Christmas

Her Convenient Cowboy

Her Cowboy Deputy

Catching the Cowgirl

The Cowboy's Honor

Winning the Schoolmarm

The Wrangler's Ready-Made Family

Christmas Homecoming

Heart of Gold

Sutter's Hollow series (contemporary romance)

His Small-Town Girl

Secondhand Cowboy

The Cowgirl Next Door

Cowboy Fairytales series (contemporary fairytale romance)

Once Upon a Cowboy

Cowboy Charming

The Toad Prince

The Beastly Princess

The Lost Princess

Kissing Kelsey

Courting Carrie

Stealing Sarah

Keeping Kayla

Melting Megan

The Other Princess

The Prince's Matchmaker

Hometown Sweethearts series (contemporary romance)

Kissed by a Cowboy

Love Letters from Cowboy

Mistletoe Cowboy

The Bull Rider

The Brother

The Prodigal

Cowgirl for Keeps

Jingle Bell Cowgirl

Heart of a Cowgirl

3 Days with a Cowboy

Prodigal Cowgirl

Soldier Under the Mistletoe

The Nanny's Christmas Wish

The Rancher's Unexpected Gift

Someone Old

Someone New

Someone Borrowed

Someone Blue (newsletter subscribers only)

Ten Dates

Next Door Santa

Always a Bridesmaid

Love Lessons

Not in a Series

Wagon Train Sweetheart (historical romance)

Printed in Great Britain
by Amazon